Dakota Rage

Chance Lawton lived with his best friend, Ishna-Kobay, amongst a Nakota Sioux tribe in the Black Hills of Dakota. They hunted and broke mustangs – until a fake army patrol ambushed them, stole their belongings and killed Ishna-Kobay.

Lawton usually liked to steer clear of trouble, but avenging his friend's murder was no trouble: the way he saw it, it was his bounden duty. And if duty meant facing 'Captain' Brodie Hall's guns, then so be it. . . .

Dakota Rage

Jake Douglas

A Black Horse Western

ROBERT HALE · LONDON

© Jake Douglas 2011
First published in Great Britain 2011

ISBN 978-0-7090-9103-5

Robert Hale Limited
Clerkenwell House
Clerkenwell Green
London EC1R 0HT

www.halebooks.com

Typeset by
Derek Doyle & Associates, Shaw Heath
Printed and bound in Great Britain by
CPI Antony Rowe, Chippenham and Eastbourne

CHAPTER 1

THE PATROL

They were waiting for him as he drove the bunch of fifteen half-broke mustangs through Cradle Pass. The Nakota Sioux, on his sturdy-looking paint, brought up the drag, seemingly unbothered by the shrouding dust.

The welcoming committee, a ragged army patrol, stayed well hidden. Only after the mustanger appeared riding his big sorrel, half-visible in the dust, did they show themselves.

Ten men closed in behind from the left, careful to make sure they had the Indian between them and the mustangs. Chance Lawton glimpsed a captain's uniform up front as four more riders cut across, startling the mustangs and forcing them into a small arroyo, hazing them on with loud yells.

He reined down fast, hand dropping to his six-gun, but the captain confronted him, one hand raised.

5

'Don't touch it if you want to live.'

That was plain enough, seeing as most of the soldiers were now pointing their rifles in his direction, so he took his hand away from the gun, employed it with the other hand, plus his knees, to help quieten down the nervous sorrel.

'Got some spirit left in him, I see,' opined the, captain, in a voice that had a harsh edge: from too much tobacco, or alcohol, maybe. 'I like that in a hoss.'

'Not worth a spent cartridge you take all the backbone out of 'em,' Lawton agreed. He was a rangy man who sat a saddle so easy he seemed like one of the fabled centaurs. He looked steadily at the army man. 'We got some sort of problem here, Cap'n?'

' "We" haven't. Just you. If your name's Lawton.'

The trail man nodded almost imperceptibly, waiting now.

'Who's the Injun?' asked a rangy lieutenant, positioned off to one side of the grey-haired eaptain. 'Looks half asleep.'

'Only seems that way. His name's Ishna-Kobay, he's a Nakota Sioux. He helps me out now and again.' He lifted his voice slightly. 'See if you can settle 'em down, Mo.'

The Indian moved his horse around an armed soldier, who stiffened in the saddle as the Indian made for the entrance to the arroyo. The mustangs were restless, moving back and forth. The soldier called, 'Lieutenant. . . ?'

Grim-faced, the officer nodded curtly. 'Watch him.'

6

Lawton turned to the captain. 'What's the problem, Cap'n? And "Captain Who" . . . if I might ask.'

'You might. Brodie Hall, Captain, Second/Seventh Cavalry, or as much of it as has been reformed since Custer's foolishness. My patrol area takes in the Black Hills here, and you're riding out of them with a bunch of horses. I figure I'm due an explanation.'

Lawton frowned, watching as much as he could see of the Indian riding around the mustangs. 'I'm Lawton.'

The captain frowned, showing a trace of annoyance. 'Gonna make me do this the hard way, I see. *Who* Lawton?'

'Chance Lawton.'

'Well, you're not from around here with that accent. How far south?'

'West Virginia. But not for a long time.'

'Hmmmm. "Chance": now that sounds like it could have an interesting story attached to it.'

Lawton shrugged. 'Couple immigrants searching for Manifest Destiny found me wandering in the wilderness. I was buck naked and about three years old. Never did find anyone within a day's ride who'd own up to being my folks, so they took me in, raised me.'

The captain half-smiled as he nodded. 'They took a "chance". Yes, I see. All right. What're you doing here, coming out of these hills with those horses?'

'That's what I've been doing – hunting broncs.'

'In the Black Hills?'

'There's a slew of mustangs in there, you know

7

where to look.'

'That all you were looking for? Mustangs?'

Lawton sighed. 'Think I savvy this now. No, I haven't been searching for gold, Cap'n. Too hard to find and pays too little for all that effort. I chase down green horses, break 'em to the halter, then sell to the Cavalry at Fort Savage.'

Lawton waited out the officer, who seemed angry now as if he wasn't being shown due respect. His voice was bleak.

'You're only a drifter then? No steady work?'

'It's steady enough once I start. But I like to do a job, get paid for it, take a rest, and when the money's low, I go look for more. I don't mind hard work, but I like it best when it's outdoors.'

'Sounds like ex-convict talk to me, Cap'n; the way they dream.' The lieutenant with the axe-blade face sitting his mount beside his superior officer moved his thin upper lip when he spoke so that he gave the appearance of sneering. 'Show us your hands, drifter.'

Lawton made no move to comply, his hands staying folded on the saddle horn.

Lieutenant Abe McCracken flushed. 'Cap'n. . . ?'

Captain Hall jerked his head at Lawton. 'Obey.'

Lawton turned his palms up and McCracken put his mount alongside, reached for one hand – the right one – but Lawton pulled it back. They locked gazes and the lieutenant smiled thinly. 'Touchy, huh? Look at them calluses – that kinda trough at their base, right across the hand. Only one thing'll do that, Cap'n: the hickory handle of a rock-pile sledge.'

He sneered triumphantly, and Lawton, not looking away, said, 'Rope running through your hand trying to drag a mustang that's half-brother to a twister into the nubbing-post'll do it better. Don't mean one of the plaited grass lassos like most cowhands use, but braided rawhide, which is what I use.'

The lieutenant spat contemptuously. 'Fast thinker this one, Cap'n!'

The captain nodded slowly, studying Lawton more closely now, noting his work-worn clothes, the rifle-butt colour of his face and hands, dusty stubble, long, dark hair showing untidily under the battered hat, and the clear, steady, unafraid blue eyes in the narrow face, the slightly prominent cheekbones. A hint of Indian blood, maybe?

'You've been on a chain-gang, mister,' accused Hall.

'If I had, I'd've had a bellyful of the great outdoors, I reckon.'

'Don't you sass the cap'n like that!' the lieutenant snapped, moving restlessly in his saddle, but settling down when Hall lifted a gloved hand.

'Think I've heard of you, Lawton. Injun-lover, guide or something?'

Lawton shook his head. 'No. But I trap mustangs in the spring, hunt bear, any bison that might've strayed on to the plains, beaver, fox, come winter. Long as it's got fur and I can make a dollar from it.'

The lieutenant spat. 'He's a no-account drifter all right, Cap'n. A real live saddlebum.'

'I'm obliged to no man, Lieutenant. I pay my debts, in cash or kind, and live the way I want to.'

'With Injuns!' the lieutenant said, gesturing to the colourful saddle-blanket on the sorrel. 'You don't see the likes of that in the market place. That's tribal, top notch, too. You steal it?'

'Given to me by Chief Redfoot. I broke in a paint pony for his youngest son. If you're interested, he got his name from wading through the blood of the warriors he'd killed in battle.'

'So, you *do* live with the Indians!' snapped Hall.

'Stay with 'em, sometimes – never for long. Do a little trading.'

'Like horses – for gold?'

Lawton's level gaze swung to the lieutenant. 'No.'

They waited for more but the mustanger offered nothing. 'We're going to have to search your gear,' Captain Hall said officiously. 'Climb down and stand over there against the rocks.'

Lawton's grey eyes narrowed. 'I know all about the army's panic over gold being here, Cap'n. They've banned whites from going into the Black Hills, afraid if there's a big gold strike it'll cause a rush – which'd mean more trouble with the Indians, naturally. The army's stretched to the limit already and wouldn't be able to cope. Am I right?'

'If you know that, why go into the Black Hills at all?' growled McCracken, watching the arroyo now as the Nakota Indian rode across the entrance confining the horses. He yelled abruptly, spun his mount and brought up his Remington .44 pistol: 'Watch that Injun! He's tryin' to escape!'

Heads were still turning to look at the startled

Ishna-Kobay when Lieutenant McCracken's pistol bucked twice in his hands, the gunshots slapping back from the walls of the pass.

The Sioux fell clumsily from the saddle, rolled once in the dust – then the panicked horses drove over him.

There was a sudden grating cry, coming from deep in the throat, and McCracken snapped his head around, startled, as Lawton's big sorrel rammed forward and collided with his horse. Animals and men went down in a tangle of raking hoofs, flying hats and limbs.

The captain moved his own startled mount back quickly and soldiers close by did the same. Before anyone could act, Chance Lawton hurled himself at the lieutenant as he staggered to his feet. Their bodies collided and Lawton smashed a fist into McCracken's face, drove a knee into his belly, picked the man up bodily, with a loud grunt of effort, and hurled him into the rocks.

Then two soldiers rode in. Rifle butts slammed down and Lawton staggered, knees folding as he sat heavily, shaking his head, blood trickling down his dark face.

'Stay put!' snapped the captain as Lawton tried, unsuccessfully, to get up. 'By God, you're hair-trigger! And you're in a heap of trouble, Lawton. Attacking an officer who was carrying out his duty.'

'Cold-blooded murder is what it was!' Lawton's words were a little slurred and he shook his buzzing head, trying to clear it. 'Mo wasn't trying to do anything but calm the mustangs, and this trigger-happy son of a bitch—'

'Enough! We all saw what happened. I'm sorry if you've lost a friend, Lawton, but we can't afford to have our authority flouted. You ought to know that. So you hunt horses in the forbidden Black Hills. What do you do with them?'

Lawton was still dazed, didn't want to let this go, but surrounded by so many hostiles, he said, after a long pause, 'I've a sort of open contract with Colonel Helm at Fort Savage. He'll take whatever horses I bring in. We dicker some over the price but he mostly likes the broncs I deliver.'

Hall's eyes narrowed and he twitched his grey-streaked moustache, sniffing. 'This "arrangement" you have is with *Colonel* Helm?'

'Colonel Joshua Helm. He'd be hardly able to walk if he was the kind to wear all his medals at once. You must know him, Cap'n?'

'Heard of him.' Clipped tones, dismissive. Then, 'There wouldn't be an army man north of the Red River who hasn't. He's a friend of yours, I take it?'

Chance Lawton shrugged. 'We do business together.'

'Thought the cap'n told you to go stand over yonder?' cut in McCracken, pointing his Remington pistol at Lawton now with one hand, the other holding a wadded kerchief against his bleeding nose. Hunched against his body's pain, his eyes blazed death when he looked at the mustanger.

'Do as he says,' Hall snapped. The mustanger took his time, but walked over to the rocks, wiping a little

12

blood from his face.

While they searched his gear – and didn't bother repacking his bedroll or saddle-bags – Lawton squatted and built a cigarette, smoked slowly, watching closely, eyes straying several times to the dusty body of the Sioux lying at the arroyo's entrance.

'You won't find any gold,' he said once when Hall glowered at him.

'Is that a challenge of some sort?'

Lawton shook his head slowly: he couldn't believe this cavalry captain; the man was on the prod, enough to condone the killing of Ishna-Kobay. And he seemed to be Hall's target. He couldn't help but wonder why? They'd never met before, though he had heard of Hall and his punitive patrols, hunting down Indians and what he called white renegades in the Black Hills.

But he had a notion way back in his mind that the army had dismissed Hall and his patrols for unnecessary brutality. Which would make this deal . . . unofficial.

A few minutes later the lieutenant shook his head, looking disappointed. But he brightened when the captain said,

'Just as well for you, Lawton. However, we'll be confiscating your horses.'

The mustanger came to his feet so fast that McCracken had to fumble to bring up his Remington and cover him. 'Stay put!'

Lawton froze, his gaze icy now. 'I worked my butt off for weeks trapping and breaking those broncs. I aim to sell 'em to Colonel Helm, like I said . . . and he'll get a full report about Mo's murder.'

'Why you call that Injun crowbait "Mo"?' demanded McCracken.

Lawton was going to ignore him but said, 'He likes – liked – molasses.' Let them figure it out from that.

'You're out of luck this time, Lawton,' the captain said. 'We've been hearing about your trespassing in the Black Hills for some time. You know damn well it's against territorial law, and I'm bound to enforce it here in South Dakota and elsewhere. There's no *colonel* here to help you, so don't push your luck. I'm confiscating these horses. I could manacle you, drag you back to Fort Lansing, and see you put on trial. You'd be able to add to those calluses then.'

It seemed to be a good joke, judging by the laughter of Lieutenant McCracken and some of the soldiers.

There were too many guns pointing his way for Lawton to do anything but stand there and watch. Looked like they were going to at least leave him the sorrel. . . . *No!*

'I like your saddle, feller,' McCracken said abruptly. 'All them conchos – silver, too. Mex, huh? Tell you what, providin' the cap'n agrees, I'll swap you my army-issue McClellan saddle for yours. OK?'

'Keep your hands off my gear,' Lawton warned softly.

McCracken pursed his lips and widened his eyes. 'Oooooh! Ain't that a scary voice! Cap'n, do I have your permission to swap with this saddlebum?'

'Can't think of any regulation off the top of my

14

head that'd make me say "no", Lieutenant, so. . . .'
Hall gestured vaguely in the sorrel's direction. 'You go
ahead, and if I do come up with something, why we'll
worry about it then.' He smiled crookedly at the mustanger. 'Be kinda late for you, but that's the way the
cards fall, you walk that thin line between the law and
breaking it.'

Lawton, tight-lipped, glanced towards the ragged,
blood-stained body of Ishna-Kobay lying in the arroyo
entrance.

McCracken started forward, a little warily, watching
Lawton's cold eyes following his every movment. He
quickly removed the army saddle from his chestut and
dumped it at the man's feet. He watched for a
moment and when Chance didn't move, skirted him
and went to the sorrel.

'Maybe I'll just take hoss and all. Save me unsad-
dlin' then saddlin' up again. I want that blanket
anyway. OK by you, drifter?'

'Better you don't try it, Lieutenant.'

McCracken snorted and the moment his hands
reached for the sorrel's reins Lawton lunged, grabbed
the grubby collar of McCracken's uniform jacket and
hurled him backwards. The lieutenant couldn't keep
balance, slammed into a rock, grunted as air was
driven from him. He fell to his knees. Lawton was in
front of him in a flash, fists looping in from first the
right hand side, then the left. The lieutenant's head
swivelled from side to side and as his body toppled
Captain Hall called for his men to close in.

Chance spun to meet them, pulled his Colt from

leather and slammed it across the head of the first man to reach him. He swiped backhanded and caught a second soldier in the face. A third lunged in, tried to knock the Colt from his grip but stumbled.

Lawton, swaying, stomped on his instep and then they were all over him, fists sledging and hammering, knees, boots, and, eventually, rifle butts, jarring his lean frame.

In seconds he was driven down, stretched out on the ground, bloody, fighting for breath. Then McCracken's heavy army boot slammed against the side of his head and he fell off the planet amongst whirling stars until they finally burned out and there was nothing but blackness.

The first thing he saw when he opened his eyes and the misty veils cleared sufficiently, was Lieutenant's McClellan saddle lying in the dust a few feet away.

Coming out of his daze slowly, he concentrated on the black leather saddle. It was lightweight, utilitarian, designed by a man who knew the benefit of such things from long experience: Captain George A. McClellan. The seat was narrow but deep, the front and back curving higher than normal, supporting a man's lower back and pelvic muscles, which would be affected by long hours riding patrol. There was no rifle scabbard, just an adjustable leather ring to slip the barrel of the army-issue Trapdoor Springfield rifle through. There was a sabre ring on the other side, a wide cinch strap, and adjustable stirrups with broad leather backing to save the mount's hide from continual rubbing.

A man who knew his business, George A. McClellan.

'At least I'm able to think clearly enough, so maybe my skull isn't busted wide open, after all – but it sure as hell feels that way. . . .'

Just inside the arroyo, Lane saw McCracken's army mount cropping grass contentedly, happily relieved of its burden of both rider and saddle, reins trailing.

The Indian's broken body had been dragged into the edge of the rock field. There were flies buzzing around it already.

Grim-faced now, Lawton leaned against a boulder, staring at the man who had been his companion on so many mustang chases, quiet as Indians usually were around white men, even those they shared beans and coffee with.

Somehow, he was going to have to force himself to his feet and give Ishna-Kobaya decent burial, his face turned towards the Great Spirit and the rising sun as he would wish. That ledge halfway up the mountain seemed ideal.

Then he would have to catch McCracken's mount, throw the McClellan on and ride . . . where?

Holding his throbbing head, feeling half-congealed blood from a gash caused by a rifle butt, he felt his aching ribs and sore belly. Despite these injuries, he figured it oughtn't to be too hard to trail Captain Brodie Hall – not with his patrol pushing that bunch of half-broke mustangs. They'd leave a trail like a road in the wilderness.

Colonel Helm would help, but it was a long way to

Fort Savage, and there were plenty of other places between here and there where Hall's patrol could go.

But wherever they had gone, he would go, too.

Count on it.

Breathless, after forcing himself through the exhausting chores he had set himself, he sat back in the half-shade, eyes closed, legs straight out in front, letting the pain take over for a spell. He hurt plenty but it gave him something to fight, get his blood racing again. . . .

He would be on the trail by sundown.

But when he tried to stand up, his legs wavered and he had to grasp the rock for support.

He wasn't quite ready – but that was OK.

Chance Lawton was a patient man.

CHAPTER 2

CHEYENNE CROSSING

He had heard of Cheyenne Crossing – nothing good, either – but he'd never ridden over the state line into Wyoming to visit. Actually, the town straddled the line, being partly in Wyoming, partly in South Dakota.

Law was in short supply in both places.

This was where the long trail had led him: down south to Hot Springs, south again to the Fall River, and the big lake, where he learned the horses had been sold to traders who were heading deep into Dakota Territory, as far as the foothills of the Black Hills, anyway.

Sure, just the foothills!

Like hell! Those broncs would be traded off to the Indians for a good slice of the gold that was said to exist in that area, though the army would never admit it. They labelled it 'Forbidden Territory' on their geological survey maps. If the Indians were being used as slave labour by white renegades to mine any gold, the army didn't want to know about it. If it wasn't 'official', ignore it.

So the horses were gone, or most of them. They'd told him the lieutenant was still riding a big sorrel with a concha-studded Mexican saddle: Chance's private mount, and probably not recoverable. But the lieutenant had to be found. The men who had stolen the mustangs hadn't disappeared off the face of the earth. He would find them; he had the expertise and the motive.

Still, it took him almost two weeks of hot, dusty hungry trails to lead him eventually to Cheyenne Crossing.

It was a scattered town; some buildings already weathered grey, others had not yet lost their yellowish fresh-sawn-lumber look entirely. A variety of folk walked the boardwalks or rode the streets, clattered by in flatbed wagons. Some watched him narrowly, others with a touch of fear, in case it was some badge-toter checking out his Wanted dodgers, maybe? Others showed just plain old curiosity for the arrival of yet another stranger.

One of the first things he learned while stabling McCracken's horse was that the sheriff was named Hall, Jude Hall – and. . . ?

'Yeah, he has a brother who's a captain in the cavalry,' the livery man told him readily enough. 'Not sure, but he might be thinking of retiring. I know he's been lookin' for a place out near the river fork. Dunno what he's usin' for money 'cause it's sure expensive out that way and . . . say! Here's the sheriff now. Ask him yourself. Jude! Feller here askin' after the captain.'

Sheriff Jude Hall was a big, heavy-shouldered man whose head seemed too small for his bulk. His face was broad, like Lawton remembered Captain Brodie Hall's, and he sported a droopy frontier moustache, too, stained brown underside from tobacco smoke. There was a vertical scar between his eyes which were deepset under bony ridges. What Dakota could see of them looked mean. Just like the captain's. . . .

The lawman walked with a swagger, his head cocked a little on one side: arrogant, confident, *don't mess with me.*

'Someone said a rider just came in forkin' a hoss with a McClellan saddle and army brand on the withers, but he looked like a civilian. What happened to your uniform, feller? Don't tell me you don't have one.'

'I don't have one.'

Jude displayed a row of stained teeth, briefly. 'Then you gonna have to tell me why you're forkin' an army hoss. You could be a deserter for all I know.'

'Why don't you ask your brother.'

'Who? Lacy? He wouldn't know nothin'.'

'Hell, I meant the captain. How many "Halls" are there around here, anyway?'

'Whole slew of us, but don't you worry none about that. You got a name?'

Lawton told him and the sheriff's cocky grin widened.

'Well, now, fancy that. Chance Lawton. Just the feller my big brother Brodie asked me to keep a lookout for. You recollect Brodie. Cap'n of cavalry. . . ?'

'Him and Lieutenant McCracken, whose horse, incidentally, this happens to be. He took—'

Jude held up a hand, smile gone, looked quickly at the livery man. 'You're my witness, Robbie. You heard him admit he was ridin' an army hoss, one just like Lieutenant Abe McCracken reported to me as stolen not five days ago.'

The livery man shuffled his feet uncomfortably at the sheriff's words. 'Well, I ain't sure he said that. . . .'

The lawman ignored him. There was a six-gun in his hand now Lawton hadn't even seen him draw. He quickly lifted his hands out from his sides.

'Hold up, Sheriff! I didn't steal any horse. McCracken swapped this one here for mine, a big sorrel—'

'Swapped? Damn you, mister, don't you try to hornswoggle me! Why would he *swap* an army hoss for your jughead, whatever it was? It's agin the law, and could get him shot, or a stretch in an army stockade. You just lift them hands a little higher and turn around slow while I take your six-gun. Then you an' me are walkin' down to the jail. Got a nice clean cell all ready an' waitin' for you.'

Covered by the Colt, Lawton's eyes were hooded now and what was showing of them looked mighty bleak. He lifted his hands and turned slowly.

Suddenly the sheriff stepped forward and kicked him savagely in the back of the left thigh.

'Take it easy, Jude!' gasped the startled livery man. 'I mean. . . .'

Lawton went down hard on one knee and a boot in the back shoved him face first into the stall wall. Dazed, he felt his six-gun taken from his holster, and he knew Jude Hall must be leaning over him.

So he came up with a roar and the top of his head smashed squarely into the lawman's face. Hall grunted aloud in shock and pain, staggered back, dropping Lawton's gun, his own wavering wildly.

Staggering slightly, Lawton scooped up his Colt. By then Jude Hall was straightening groggily, face bloody. He looked dazed but was reacting by instinct, reaching for Lawton, grabbing his left arm and spinning the man roughly into the wall of the stall again. He crowded in, using his weight to pin the mustanger, but Lawton squirmed and got his gun arm free, swiped at the lawman with his Colt. It was a cramped motion and lacked sting, but was hard enough to make the sheriff rear back as the barrel raked across his forehead, starting more blood flowing into his eyes.

Half-blinded, Jude Hall was cursing and gritting obscenities now as he lurched in, trying to keep the mustanger pinned against the wall. Lawton ducked under the groping arm, came up right against the man and rammed the gun barrel hard and deep into Hall's midriff. The lawman gagged, stumbled back as breath rushed out of him, and he started to bend.

Lawton brought up a knee, felt pain as the kneecap crashed into the bony forehead, and then lurched aside as Hall sprawled in the walkway between the stalls.

Robbie McCall, the livery man, frowned, looking at Lawton warily. 'You're in a heap of trouble, feller.'

'My middle name, but it's nothing to what you'll be if you don't saddle my mount for me, pronto.'

Robbie lifted his hands. 'I don't want no trouble.'

He started to cinch the McClellan saddle in place and twisted to watch as Lawton walked to where several saddles were piled in a corner. Two of them still had rifles in the scabbards and he slid the nearest gun free, examined it. A Winchester .44, the popular range-rider's longarm, in reasonable condition, but could stand some attention.

'That'll be too loose in the saddlering of that there McClellan,' the livery man said, pausing in his chore. 'Barrel ain't thick enough for the ring to grip. I can throw in a reg'lar saddle, instead of the McClellan, if you want.'

Lawton's face showed brief suspicion, then he nodded. 'I'm obliged. But you're making more trouble for yourself.'

McCall glanced down at the bloody, unconscious sheriff. 'The Halls run this place. 'Fact, the cap'n is thinkin' of changin' its name to "Hallmark". Mostly they don't give none of us non-Halls a decent shake. 'Fact is, the cap'n is that in name only. Army retired him, but some of his old crew stayed with him. Once in a while they dust off the old uniforms and . . . well, you've had a sample of what they get up to.'

Lawton stared hard. 'You *like* trouble for yourself?'

'Well, I blab a bit too much, I guess. Be obliged if you'd tie me up before you go?'

Lawton smiled thinly. 'I can do that, long as you tell me where I'll find the captain and that murdering snake of a Lieutenant McCracken.'

Robbie McCall shook his head. 'Dunno where McCracken is for sure; somewheres outta town. Been known to hang out in the hills, at a kinda unofficial settlement there; a place they call The Post on account it's got a kinda tradin' post there. Mostly they trade in cattle with changed brands and guns with worn firin' pins they can pass on to the Injuns, stuff like that. Cap' n Hall's got a house south of town.' He sniffed and made an attempt at a snooty accent. 'The better part of town, you know. . . ?'

Jude Hall started to stir, lifting a hand to his throbbing head. McCall's eyes widened. 'Hell! He's comin' round!'

Lawton casually kicked Hall in the head. 'You got some rope?' As Robbie nodded and turned away, swallowing nervously, Lawton said, 'Better make this look good.'

McCall turned back to say something. But a big fist crammed the words back into his mouth.

It was almost sundown when Lawton pulled out of Cheyenne Crossing, the shadows long and deep in the narrow streets. He rode through these, staying away from the wide better-lighted boundaries of Main, found his way behind business buildings and then through bunches of scattered houses. Some were still in the process of construction, with the owners living in the one or two rooms so far completed.

He made for the river and followed it south, passing the edge of town, with only one or two cabins and one junk-built shack, which was in darkness.

A little further along, he saw a two-storeyed house and smelled the linseed oil they had soaked the clapboards with. There was paint around two of the front windows and the door was a dark colour, maybe bottle-green. There was lace at the windows, drapes, too, dimly lighted by several lamps inside. The picket fence was white, with the palings tipped with a dark colour which probably matched the door or window frames.

Getting into a richer area of town now.

McCall had said Captain Brodie Hall's place was three-parts completed. It sat on the rise just above the river bend, the land at least several acres with planted shade-trees and a brush awning along the length of the western wall: what they would call a *ramada* in Arizona or New Mexico.

He reined down in a clump of trees. It gave him a good view of the big house which already had two gables. It looked like a third was under construction. There were lights showing downstairs and there might be one upstairs at a window with heavy drapes, too, or just a candle burning, not throwing much light against the cloth.

So, Captain Hall was home, or some of his kinfolk or servants were.

Lawton draped the reins of the buckskin he had taken from the livery, with McCall's consent, though the man would howl and moan that it had been stolen, just to make himself look good to the Halls when he was found and released, then he slid the Winchester from the sloping saddle scabbard.

He walked quietly around the house, able to look into two rooms. One was a large kitchen where two Indian women worked, one scrubbing dishes in a cut-down cask, the second preparing vegetables at a wooden table. The other window showed the captain's den or office. He seemed to be alone, wore half-moon glasses almost on the tip of his broad nose, and was reading some papers, occasionally frowning. He wore civilian shirt and trousers, and a pair of felt slippers: at his ease.

But he almost fell out of his chair when Lawton slammed the outside door open and stepped inside, swiftly moving to his left, and pushed the door closed behind him.

'What in tarnation d'you th—' The captain, half-out of his chair, stopped in mid-word as he recognized Lawton. He sank back, set the papers on the small table beside his chair; they rustled because his hand was shaking. He whipped off the spectacles, blinking as the rifle barrel pointed steadily at him.

'Well, you took your time. Expected you days ago.'

He sounded calm enough but his hands had trouble staying still, wandered across his belly, fingers tapped on the arm of the chair.

'I'm here now.'

'And looking kind of wild and . . . upset. Just you take it easy, feller. I don't aim to hassle you. But the fact you're here must mean my young brother, Jude, is not feeling too chipper, right?'

'He'll have a headache for a while. You damn Halls are a mean lot. Like to make trouble for folks.'

The captain smiled. 'Figured that already? Well, I thought all along you had more brains than the average 'breed.'

'I don't take offence at being called a 'breed, Cap'n. It's not true, far as I know, but if it was, I'd still be me. That's all that counts.'

'Hmmmm. Well, what d'you want? I can't help you, you know. You broke the law and—'

'What damn law?'

'Dakota law. The way I administer it.'

Lawton nodded. 'Yeah, that's right enough. Think you've taken a lot more on yourself than Colonel Helm knows.'

Hall laughed briefly. 'Just reminding me about the higher-ranking officer you sell your remounts to? I haven't forgot, Lawton. But Fort Savage is a long way from here. If you were smart, you would be, too.'

'Well, I'm not too smart, Cap'n. But I'll get out of your hair soon enough. Just tell me where I can find McCracken.'

Hall sobered, nodding slowly to himself. 'Yes, I should've figured that. You want him because of the Indian. Treacle, or whatever you called him.'

'I know your memory's better'n that, Cap'n. You won't rile me by miscalling his name. . . . He's happy

28

wherever hs is; his spirit has found a home.'

'My God! You actually believe that stuff?'

'He did, that's what matters.'

Hall shook his head slowly. 'Miserable-looking man – barely spoke. Don't think I heard him more than grunt.'

'His way – when he had nothing to say, he said nothing. Some whites could've learned a lesson or two from Mo.'

'I'm *sure* you're part Indian!'

Lawton shrugged. 'Mebbe it's just that I've been around 'em a lot. Now, let's get back to McCracken.'

Hall pursed his lips, shook his head slowly. 'No, I don't think so. I don't know for sure where he is in any case. Tell me, what will you do if I don't give you the information you want? I have men I can call, you know—'

Lawton didn't hesitate: he took a vesta from his shirt pocket, snapped it into life with a horny thumbnail, and stepped over to the main window with the velvety drapes. Captain Hall was already standing up by his chair, face white and alarmed as Lawton held the flame an inch from the dangling cord and tassle.

'Call your men. But they better come mighty quick, and bring lots of water.'

'Now you wait! My God! *Wait*! Please!' He was sweating, short of breath. 'I didn't mean to beg. But – but I will if that's what it takes! This is my future home and my wife and family will be moving in here shortly. Just – lower that match and we'll talk.'

Lawton stamped the flame out beneath his boot.

'I've got a pocketful of 'em, Cap'n, remember that. This is a nice place, but I hear you're looking at land out at the river forks. Rich man's territory.'

Captain Hall frowned, his mouth tightening under his moustache. 'Someone's been talking out of turn!'

'They tell me it's prime land out there. A man needs a decent bank balance to even get started. More than the miserable army pension.'

Hall had composed his face now, sober, only mildly interested.

'How's your bank balance, Cap'n?'

'For one thing, it's none of your business. But . . . it's healthy enough for the small investment I thought I'd make; secure something worthwhile for my family's future.'

'Good thoughts. But on a captain's pay? I mean, even out here in the wilderness, making allowances for all the extras, it's not that great. You couldn't've saved much.'

Hall seemed very wary now, spoke slowly, choosing his words carefully. 'Perhaps you have been mis-informed – or perhaps it's merely that I have been circumspect, canny with my spending. *And* perhaps my wife has money of her own, to help me with my proposed invesment.'

Lawton smiled thinly. 'Got all the answers, huh? I passed through three different army posts before I came here. Might come as a surprise to you, but your colleagues don't think much of you, not as a man, or a soldier – which you are *not* any longer – or in your other dealings. I won't go into them, except to say a lot seem mighty suspect.'

'Damn you!' Hall's face was darkening now. 'Get out of my house! I don't have to sit here and be insulted like this! I don't even know what you're implying.'

'Oh? Didn't I make it clear? I was wondering whether, somehow, you'd come into a deal of money since I last saw you in the Black Hills. . . ?'

Hall stared blankly, then suddenly laughed. 'My God, you should be in a medicine show! You're a damn good comedian – in your sly way.'

'Maybe it's just an Indian sense of humour. But let's get back to brass tacks; you were going to tell me where I can find McCracken.'

Hall sagged down into his chair, swallowing, pale now, but striving to stay in command of the situation, which was getting way too far out of hand. His voice was hoarse when he spoke. 'You're a fool going after him! He only did his duty, shot a prisoner trying to escape. No blame can be laid upon him.'

'*I* blame him. Ever seen a man trying to hobble around with a foot mangled by a bullet, Cap'n?'

Lawton's gun came up and the hammer notched back, the barrel pointing at Hall's slippered feet.

'I-I can only tell you where he might be!'

'Then do it.'

CHAPTER 3

OUTPOST

Lawton didn't let on to Captain Hall that he knew the man was lying when he gave him directions how to find The Post, the semi-legal trading post at the semi-outlaw settlement in the rugged foothills.

Robbie McCall had told him enough, so that he knew the outpost lay more to the west than Captain Hall had claimed; higher up, too, though the directions weren't specific. The army man had said earlier that he had men he could call upon to help him, and Lawton figured that that was what the shrewd captain had in mind in giving him wrong information.

It was likely good ambush country – Hall was sending him into it and would likely have a couple of his hardcases waiting for him.

Lawton couldn't waste time; there was the beginning of an afterglow and he wanted to be in the dark hills as soon as possible. He left town by a trail that would lead him in the direction Brodie Hall had given him, knowing damn well he would be watched. As soon as the captain was sure he was following his directions he would send gunmen after him.

He could read the stars easily enough and meandered for a while to give them a chance to start their nightly display. He studied them briefly, especially the one called Cassiopeia, and then the Dog Star, Sirius, recognized and revered by the Indians. Some tribes believed their distant ancestors actually came from that bright star and worshipped it as the home of the Great Spirit.

Be that as it may, he used it to point his way; he made a snaking trail through dark arroyos and came to a high walled narrow pass, a perfect place for an ambush.

Only *he* would be the one waiting with a rifle. . . .

He was wrong.

Captain Hall, or the men he dispatched, were smarter than Lawton had allowed. No doubt knowing the country well, they had gone straight to the point of ambush while he meandered more or less aimlessly, acting like a man not sure of his directions, and were waiting for Chance Lawton to appear.

When he entered the pass, searching for a way up to a ledge or high place he could shoot from, he didn't realize that he and his mount were silhouetted against a pale background of sandstone.

The first shot almost nailed him.

He actually saw the muzzle-flash of the rifle, way up there on the ledge he had chosen for himself. At almost the same instant he felt the air-whip of the bullet passing his left ear.

Instinct drove him to the right, snatching the rifle from his saddle scabbard. As he left the saddle he kicked the horse hard. It whinnied and lurched, half-reared, adding to the confusion so that the man above couldn't be sure where his target had gone.

Lawton hit hard but landed in a sandy spot, and though his crashing body kicked up a fan of light-coloured dust it didn't help the bushwhacker. The man triggered three fast shots, raking the area; the slugs zipped into the sand with squeaky sounds, one ricocheting from a rock, spraying stone chips.

Lawton heaved up, threw himself behind a low line of rocks and, panting, squirmed around to settle himself, his rifle already angling up towards the shooter's ledge.

Then the second man put in his two cents' worth.

He must have been almost directly above Lawton's position, for the two bullets drove straight down between the rocks and the mustanger's body.

Lawton, startled, instinctively rolled on to his back, swinging the rifle around in time to catch the muzzle-flash from another shot right up on the lip of the pass. Something blurred briefly across the blazing stars as the man shifted position slightly.

It was all Lawton needed.

The lever and trigger worked so fast his trio of shots blended into one long blast. He heard a ricochet, thought he saw rock chips fly from the edge, but it could have been an illusion – the light wasn't that good.

But he saw the killer plainly enough as the lead hammered into him, lifting his upper body violently from below. He definitely heard the man's half-grunt, half-scream of agony, then the dry-gulcher's rifle clattered down the face of the pass wall, followed a few seconds later by the man himself.

He thudded suddenly at the same time as the other gunman on the ledge shouted, 'You lousy son of a *bitch*! You've killed my brother!'

'Hope he was a Hall,' Lawton couldn't resist shouting back as he changed position fast, snaking along behind the low rocks. His belly hit the ground as a fusillade of lead raked the rocks and hard-packed earth around him, sending his hat skidding; he hoped the horse had had enough sense to find shelter.

The man up there had emptied his rifle. Through the dying echoes Chance Lawton could hear him frantically reloading, a string of curses accompanying the action, and no doubt hindering him as the surge of anger shook his frame.

Lawton was up and running; he had spotted a big boulder with an angled flat surface and he threw himself bodily behind this, rolled hard against inflexible rock and grunted as pain shot through his left shoulder.

But he clawed his way up the back of the boulder, slid his rifle ahead of him on to the flat surface, then bellied up and lay on the rock, sweating and breathing hard. He realized that the surface he was lying on was a lichen-scabbed grey in colour, and he could be seen by the rifleman, so he rolled on to his side and drew himself up to the edge, working the rifle's lever.

Just at that moment the last echo died away and, in a split second of total silence, the rifle lever's clash could be heard clearly.

He was looking at the edge, figuring the man would have moved along, closer to him. There was the movement of head and shoulders as Lawton threw the butt into his right shoulder, sighted quickly, then brought the tip of the blade foresight level with the rising sides of the buckhorn rear sight.

He pressed the butt in tightly, squeezed the trigger and felt the kick, but held the weapon steady with his grip. Almost before the first bullet chipped the edge of the ledge, he had the second on its way. It caught the man up there, just as he reared back to avoid the first slug.

There was a brief hiatus as the gunshots slapped away through the pass. Then came the clatter of the falling rifle – but no tumbling body.

He waited, a new load in the breech, finger on the trigger, cheekpiece against his face, straining to see. He heard a scraping sound, what might have been a grunt of effort, then one arm dangled over the edge, swung briefly, went still.

Lawton didn't lower the rifle, just waited. No further movement. *Make sure!*

So he fired at the dangling arm. It jerked as if kicked or yanked on a string, the flopped back. No more movement.

Good enough, so he slid back off the boulder, quickly searched for the horse and found the buckskin standing between two boulders, nibbling at a tuft of grass.

It took him twenty minutes to find a way out of the pass and up on to the high rim. He kicked a large rock over the trailing reins and, sixgun in hand now, rifle in the saddle scabbard, he made his way down to the ledge where he could see the dark, unmoving shape of Hall's man.

Lawton wiped sweat out of his eyes as he stood on the narrow strip of rock and nudged the man. He groaned a little and Lawton dropped to one knee, lugged him round. The man screamed once before Lawton propped him up against the rock. There was enough light to see the trickle of blood at one corner of his mouth, dripping from his jaw. His eyes glinted dully as he rolled his head towards Lawton.

'Y-you're – better'n – the cap'n – figured.'

'You ain't got long, *amigo*. Couple things I need to know.'

'G-g-go to – hell. . . .' There was no real force in the words, just an instinctive reply, voice weak, rasping.

'You'll be there first. You can go easy, or hard.' Lawton holstered the Colt and drew a hunting knife from a buckskin sheath, stiffened by rubbing with tree resin, at his belt. The starlight glinted off the honed steel and even the dying man could see how the blade had been worn away by constant sharpening.

The knife had had a lot of use and now the man whined as Lawton grabbed a handful of his hair at his forehead, tugging hard and lifting him an inch off the rock.

He screamed as the edge of the blade touched the stretched skin of his scalp.

'Only ever scalped one other man still alive,' Lawton said casually, making a face. 'Noisy and messy as hell. Mebbe I won't have to do it to you – *if* you tell me where McCracken is and how Brodie Hall suddenly got so much money.'

The man said nothing, staring with eyes that seemed almost ready to pop from their sockets.

But when the honed steel made the first small cut in his scalp, he started to scream. 'W-a-a-ii-i-ttt. . . !'

Lawton had learned from the dying bushwhacker that Abe McCracken was aiming to hole up at The Post, which was run by a big-bellied, small-eyed roughneck calling himself 'Beauty' Dunne. Though there was nothing beautiful about the man; he was thick-lipped, gap-toothed and balding, with a thin, yellowish scurf encrusting his pate.

Strangely, his apron was clean enough, though the clothes underneath could have done with some stone-bashing laundrying down at the small waterfall behind the main building. There were half a dozen Indian or part-Indian women there, three not yet out of their teens, two in their early twenties, and one fat squaw with a face like a buffalo who must be well into her fifties.

They were lined up under a brush awning on a small unpainted clapboard shack about ten yards from the main trading post. There was a sign in fading paint above the door:

Dunne's Dolls
Their imagination is as big
as your wallet

Lawton smiled to himself: seemed Beauty Dunne fancied himself as some kind of comic.

There were four horses at the main hitchrail, in between The Post and the girls' shack, and two at the smaller rail just past the end of The Post's veranda. Lawton tied his buckskin here, leaving the reins loose enough to slap away if he needed to leave in a hurry.

Two bearded men with hooded, suspicious eyes watched him from the rickety porch. He took his rifle from the scabbard, saw them tense slightly, then he climbed the four split-log steps, bringing him on to the same level as the men.

He nodded briefly and one, taking a dead pipe from his mouth spat a stream of brown juice over his left shoulder. It splashed alongside Lawton's left boot and the man looked up with arrogant gaze. 'Who you noddin' at? We dunno you.'

'And I dunno you. For which I'm truly thankful.' Both men frowned, not quite sure what he meant. Lawton gestured to the door of The Post. 'McCracken inside?'

Another stream of brown juice – but this time over the edge of the porch. 'Dunno no McCracken. You, Lon?'

The second man shook his head. 'Dunno as I'd want to, either.'

Lawton smiled, touched his free hand to his hat brim. 'Obliged, gents. Always like a friendly welcome.'

'You ain't gonna find it around here.'

'Guess not.' Lawton started for the door, paused as he heard the chairs scrape back, looked over his shoulder and saw both men were standing now.

One had a sawed-off shotgun which had been out of sight down beside his chair, the other had his hand on the butt of a holstered pistol. 'You ain't goin' in there.'

'That was the idea.'

'Nope. Cost you a five-spot entry fee.'

Lawton sighed. 'Hell, nothing's free these day. I'll just go in and see if I like the place. If I do, I'll pay you on the way out.'

'Hey!' bawled the one with the pipe. 'You loco? Don't you see our guns. . . ?'

'Sure.' Lawton swung his rifle up, his thumb notching the hammer back. 'See mine?'

The men glanced at each other, fighting to stifle laughter.

'Jud-uss! You b'lieve this, Lon? I got a sawed-off Greener an' he's facin' me down with a *rifle*! Who you reckon'll go down all shot to hell. . . ?'

'You might nail me, friend, but it'll be a double funeral.' The rifle was pointed right at the shotgunner's belly now. 'Lon there can mebbe say a prayer over both of us. . . .'

Lon pursed his lips, shook his head slightly at his companion. 'You're right, Bede. He's plumb loco.'

Bede nodded, jerked the shotgun towards the door. 'Aw, go on in, and see what Beauty has waitin' for you.'

Lawton nodded easily, confusing them further, and pushed inside.

It was a big room, kind of canted on one side. It had been patched with flattened kerosine tins and shingle-type pieces of wood here and there, specially on the roof; there was no ceiling and Lawton figured the warped roof would leak plenty in even a small shower of rain.

It was half-saloon, half-store, smelled of the wares of both: stale beer, the tang of brush-brewed moonshine, spices, rancid butter, leather – and sweat. There were ten men in the place, most sitting at rickety pine tables; two were at the bar, drinking from cracked glasses.

The man behind the bar – Beauty – mopped the counter in front of Lawton and nodded in friendly enough fashion.

'Welcome, stranger – long as you ain't wearin' a badge under them clothes.' He grinned, but there wasn't a lot of humour or welcome in it.

'Thanks. Reckon you must be 'Beauty', seeing as you're the best-looking man here.'

A silence, then a few chuckles. 'Don't turn your back on him, Beauty!' someone said. 'Think he's taken a shine to you!'

Lawton joined in the laughter, which died slowly when he put the rifle on the edge of the bar, but kept his right hand on the trigger, his thumb on the hammer's ear.

'No offence, Beauty, but you ain't my type. Mine runs more to men about as tall as me, mebbe a little

41

more, wolf-faced, long-haired, and goes by the name of Abe McCracken.'

There was silence in the room now and nobody was chuckling or even smiling.

'No one of that name in here, mister,' Beauty said curtly.

'Can see that. I know him by sight. Anyone tell me where he's at?'

'What'll you have?' Beauty asked, sober still, holding his washrag tight enough to make his knuckles stand out white against the grey cloth.

'Not thirsty. Only for information.'

'All out of that, stranger.'

Lawton nodded. 'Can savvy that. Might be able to spare a couple dollars for anyone can tell me where to find McCracken.'

'That ain't much for blood money,' someone announced and there were murmurings of agreement.

'Who says it's blood money?'

'Well, hell! You ain't gonna try to tell us you're gonna kiss him when you find him?'

Lawton shook his head emphatically, smiling slowly. 'I give you my word on that.'

A long silence dragged on in the room, broken only by a wheezing cough from a man at a corner table. He hawked, wiped his mouth on the ragged sleeve of his shirt. He looked middle-aged and unhealthy.

'Mister, I can use a coupla bucks, and I ain't got no love for Abe McCracken. Not one man here has, I reckon.'

'What's that got to do with it?' snapped Beauty. 'Mack's one of us – this one ain't.'

Lawton focused on the big curving thumb with the dirty nail that was thrust to within an inch of his nose across the bar. Then he reached up, snake-quick, with his left hand, seized the thumb and twisted sharply.

Beauty spun around, turning on his shoulders against his side of the bar in an effort to ease the sudden, excruciating pain. 'Christ, man! Wh-what the hell you – doin'? Ease up, goddammit! You'll break it!'

'Easy,' agreed Lawton, not letting up. His right hand swung the rifle around, the hammer cocked now, and anyone who had the notion to jump him eased back. 'I tried to be friendly. You fellers're too tough for your own good. Name's Chance Lawton, if it means anything. No? Well, that don't surprise me. But it'll mean something to McCracken, the same as his name means something to me. I've had to kill two men to get this far. I've got a full magazine in the rifle, which means if you fellers get froggy, there'll be at least eight to ten funerals – and I didn't even notice an undertaker's sign anywheres.' Beauty was still writhing trying to get his thumb free of the iron grip. 'Now all I want is to find Abe McCracken. Why, is my business. You try to make it yours, I strongly advise you start thinking about what kind of writing you'll want on your headboard. Any takers?'

The silence was as heavy as a wet blanket. Then the man with the wheezy cough stood up and took a shaky step forward.

'I ain't got long to live, anyways. You gimme five

43

bucks, mister, and I'll point you in the direction you want to go.'

'Shut up, Cass!' growled Beauty, gasping.

Lawton smiled crookedly. 'Do I get a refund if I don't find McCracken?'

The old man laughed and a couple of others gave tentative grins. A coughing bout empurpled the oldster's face and shook his thin frame. Men moved away as spittle sprayed.

'Gawd, get him outside,' growled Beauty, massaging his throbbing thumb. 'Here – Cass. Take this bottle and go drain it somewhere away from here. You, mister, you can pay me the five bucks.'

Lawton handed over the money after the coughing man nodded vigorously that he was in agreement.

The mustanger took one thin arm and steered Cass out through the rear door into the brush that grew close to the rickety old building.

'They gonna get rough with you when I'm gone, old-timer?'

The man had managed to stop coughing. He swigged from the bottle and almost went into another fit, but managed to control it. He shook his head. 'Might cuss me a little. McCracken ain't liked hereabouts. He scares folk, though. Mean bastard – what he does to them young squaws don't bear repeatin'. . . .'

'You really know where I can find him?'

'Got a good idea. Wouldn't try to trick you.'

Lawton wondered; the man had nothing to lose, the way he was right now. 'All right. I'll give you five bucks anyway. The rotgut's on me, but you better find a different kind of medicine, friend.'

'Hah! Too late for medicine. But I'll gladly take your money.'

'It's yours. Now, about Abe McCracken. . . . But first: is he still forking a big sorrel – with a Mexican saddle?'

The old man snapped his head up, his scrawny neck almost creaking. Looking somewhat puzzled, he nodded, then turned quickly as there was a brief tattoo of hoofs. Lawton saw a rider lashing his mount down slope and heading into the trees.

'You better get goin' quick, mister! Told you McCracken din' have many friends, but that's one of the few – Lonnie Bean. I'll bet my *cojones* agin a knob of goat's dung, an' hold the stakes in me mouth, that he's goin' to warn McCracken you're comin'.'

'Then I better follow Bean.'

CHAPTER 4

ABBY

'Goddammit! Couldn't you've held him?' snapped Sheriff Jude Hall, his face showing signs of his rough contact with the stable stall post and Chance Lawton's boot.

'No,' answered Captain Brodie Hall, pouring his irate brother a hefty drink. 'Get this into you: the man was on the prod. But in control. That's what you'd better do, Jude: get yourself under control.'

Jude tossed down the drink in two gulps, held out the glass for a refill. The captain obliged, smirking.

'Listen. Robbie McCall seen it all. You know what a blabbermouth he is. It'll be all over town how this damn . . . stranger – the one you told me to watch for and throw in jail – jumped me and knocked me cold! You think I want that sort of thing to get around?' He took a raging, frustrated stomp about the big parlour. 'I got enough trouble now gettin' folk to take me seriously.'

The captain waved it away. 'Calm down. *Calm down*! Dammit, Jude, get a hold of yourself. The man was too good for you, accept that.'

'The hell I will!'

Brodie Hall lifted a hand wearily. 'Just ease up a little. I know why he was here, why he's gone after Abe.'

'Hell, he's after Abe for shootin' that damn Injun!'

'Yes, that's one of the reason. But you don't need to worry. You think I liked him storming in here and holding me under a gun? Like hell. I sent Landers and Willis after him. They'll go on ahead and take care of Mr Chance Lawton.'

Jude frowned. 'We-ell, they're good boys,' he admitted slowly, but still sounded uncertain. 'But I wanted to nail that son of a bitch myself.'

'As long as he's stopped, what's it matter? No, don't answer that! It was a rhetorical question . . . I mean . . . oh, to hell with explanations! Take my word for it: by now Chance Lawton's dead, either lying somewhere he'll make a good supper for some night creature, or draped over Landers' or Willis's horse on his way back here. So why don't you sit down and relax? Your blood pressure'll kill you one of these times when you let your temper blow.'

Jude slowly sat down, sipping his second drink now.

'I'd like to be sure. . . .'

The Captain heaved a sigh. 'Then by all means "be sure"! Saddle up in the middle of the night and go see for yourself. I'm not going to have a shouting-match with you. I'm going to bed – and I assure you I will sleep well!' He turned as he opened the door. 'You'd be wise to do the same.'

'Just like Lacy! He's outta this, relaxin' with one of his women! He always manages to stay outta things, an' you an' me've gotta handle all the hassles!'

'He'll earn his keep when he's called upon,' Brodie said curtly. 'Or I'll know the reason why. Good*night*!'

Jude glowered as his elder brother left the room. Then he went to the table and poured himself another drink; the fine whiskey felt good going down. Not really relaxing him, but fanning the fires of resentment now blazing within him.

'First I've got to throw a scare into that damn Robbie McCall,' he muttered, half-aloud. 'Then, dammit! I'm gonna ride out and meet Landers and Willis – and they better be bringin' in Lawton's corpse.'

He downed the drink; then halfway through the front door paused.

'Mebbe I better take a couple of men along, just in case we have to go lookin' for Lawton. Yeah. Make up a posse, just as a precaution. . . .'

That sounded better than admitting to himself that, despite his ranting, he didn't feel at all confident about going after Chance Lawton alone.

Abe McCracken somtimes met a woman in a log cabin in a small, picturesque canyon on the Dakota side of the line.

At least, that was what the consumptive old Cass told Chance. Lawton believed him, somehow; the man had nothing to lose or gain by lying and he seemed genuinely grateful for the five dollars, plus the bottle of redeye.

'Word is she's the wife of some rancher back in the hills. Dunno how they stay in touch, but Abe manages to meet her when he wants to at the cabin. My hand's a mite shaky or I'd draw you a map. . . .'

'Just give me directions, old-timer, then go find your bed and take that bottle with you.'

The idea appealed to Cass and shortly after, Lawton rode into the night, with rifle butt on his thigh and finger on the trigger. He checked his backtrail frequently but found no sign of followers. The rider he and Cass had heard quitting town would likely reach McCracken long before Lawton could locate the mountain cabin, and would warn him, knowing these hills much better than Chance.

'Time to live up to my name,' he murmured, half-aloud, smiling thinly, setting the buckskin up a slope to a high ridge where he could see better. The starlight was backed up by a quarter-moon now, tilted in the 'spilling' position as it appeared from behind the taller peaks.

So he took his 'chance' after figuring out a couple of the landmarks Old Cass had told him to look for. He wasn't sure these would be enough to lead him to McCracken's trysting place, but an hour and a half later he saw the dark oblong of a small cabin in a small clearing, showing against the lighter grey of an almost sheer rockface.

'Knowin' McCracken for the sly son of a bitch he is,'

Cass had wheezed between coughing bouts, 'he'll have a getaway out back. Cabin's close to the rock wall and he let slip once that there's a cave or tunnel close by where he can hole up if he's surprised by the woman's husband. . . .'

On foot, rifle ready to be cocked, Lawton crouched in the brush and looked at the bulk of the cabin. There was a very small corral but no horses in it. However, he heard one stomp from the deeper shadows around the left-hand side. By shifting position he saw a brush-roofed stable. As far as he could make out there was only one horse in there, nuzzling a nosebag.

Then he froze as he heard the distinctive sound of a gun hammer cocking behind him.

A rifle muzzle pressed roughly against his spine and made him suck down a sharp breath.

'Drop that rifle and get your hands up.'

He frowned, every muscle freezing instantly.

It was a woman's voice, and she sounded calm and confident. It was so unexpected that he felt unable to move right away. The rifle's pressure screwed in harder in a gesture of impatience. He grunted softly with the stab of pain.

After a moment's more hesitation he dropped his rifle into a nearby bush and raised his hands. 'Just take it easy, lady!'

The rifle prodded. 'Move to the doorway. Sideways . . . and drag your feet!' She sounded as tense as a drawn bow.

He shuffled along the front of the cabin and

stopped when he came to the open doorway, expecting to find McCracken waiting with a shotgun. The rifle prodded him again and he took a tentative step into the darkness of the cabin.

Then the brass-bound butt of the rifle crashed against the back of his head and he fell to his knees before tumbling giddily down into a deeper blackness.

Light blinded him and made him squint as his eyelids fluttered up. He shifted his head and gasped involuntarily at pain shooting up the back of his neck and into his brain. He recognized a bullseye lantern with the circular shutter open, on a level with his face, which meant the lantern was resting on the hard-packed earthen floor.

As he tried to move light glinted off the blued steel of a rifle barrel and it tapped him on top of his head and he realized that he had lost his hat somewhere.

'God*damn*! Will you quit that? Leave my head alone.'

'What've you done with my brother?'

The question and the coldness of the words made him blink. He saw a fringed buckskin riding-skirt, tooled leather boots with small silver spurs showing beneath. Raising his eyes – painfully – he saw a white blouse mostly covered with a fringed vest that matched the skirt, above that a pale, kind of pinched face and the impression of a good mop of curly hair, dark in colour, but there wasn't enough light to make out exactly which colour: brown, black, chestnut. . . ?

'I'll do more than tap your skull for you if you've

51

harmed Wayne! Now answer my question.'

She cocked the rifle and he stiffened. 'Easy! You oughtn't cock a gun when you're all riled up like this.'

'Damn you! Never mind the lesson in firearm safety. Answer my question!'

'I dunno your brother. Nor you.'

'I'm Abby Daniels and I've found a shirt in this cabin that I gave Wayne for his last birthday – and it's got a lot of blood on it!'

He was frowning now and she allowed him to sit up slowly and lean his shoulders against the log wall. He warily took a kerchief from his pocket and held it to the back of his head. 'Be better if it was soaked in water. . . .'

'Just be thankful for small mercies – and stop stalling!'

'Lady, my name's Chance Lawton. I'm a mustanger and I work the Black Hills, sometimes with Indians. No need to look like that. I'm not the first white man to cross the "no trespass" line and I won't be the last.'

'I suppose you use the horse-hunting as a blind while you search for the gold that's supposed to be in there! And which the army don't want anyone to know about?'

'I'm no prospector.'

'Which is no answer! But never mind that. Just explain how my brother's bloodstained shirt happens to be in your cabin.'

'Not my cabin, either. *No*! Don't get more riled than you already are! I don't even know this country. I had some mustangs stolen and I'm trying to find them –

and even more, a man who killed a friend of mine during the theft.' He told her his story briefly, without mentioning specific names.

She settled, but he saw how edgy she was and he didn't feel relaxed; she held that rifle like she knew what she was doing and those long lashes covering dark eyes seemed to stand straight out in her simmering anger.

'I don't know why, but . . . I halfway believe you.'

'That's a start. Maybe enough for you to lower that damn gun hammer? It makes me nervous.'

Her full lips moved very slightly. 'All right. But you stay where you are.' She lifted the lantern to the deal table and uncovered the top so that light spilled into the cabin's only room, showing a narrow rumpled bunk in one corner, behind a grey blanket sliding along a string, a stone hearth with blackened kettle and a large pot, some packing-case cupboards screened by ragged cloth that had once been a curtain.

'I was a good way off, but I saw two men and a woman riding out of this area not long ago. In fact I've only been at the cabin for about ten minutes. I hid when I heard you zigzagging up the slope, your horse blowing.'

'Guess I pushed him a bit. I've never been here before. Had reason to believe someone had warned McCracken I was coming. He was s'posed to be with a woman.'

Nodding impatiently, she picked up a crumpled and torn blue shirt from the table. He wondered if she noticed how he tensed as he looked at the bloodstains. He couldn't help whistling softly. The sound brought her eyes snapping around to him.

'Looks like he was wounded badly.'

Tight-lipped, she nodded, then said slowly, 'There's some blood on the table here, the back of that chair opposite and on the top blanket in the bunk. I believe my brother tended to his wounds here, rested up perhaps, and now. You recognize Wayne's shirt, don't you!'

'Easy!' he said quickly as the rifle rose threateningly. 'Wayne? You said your name is "Daniels"?' She nodded, more tense now. 'When I was on my way to Cheyenne Crossing I came across a feller who'd been shot. Not hurt too bad, though he was losing a fair amount of blood. He was wearing a shirt like that. I thought he said his name was "Wade", but maybe he said "Wayne".'

She was wearing soft riding-gloves, or he was sure he would see how white her knuckles were as she gripped her rifle tighter now. Her blouse was heaving beneath the fringed buckskin vest, and he noted, casually, that she had a fine figure under there, but. . . .

'You'd better tell me about this meeting in more detail.' The tension in her voice cut like a knife.

He hesitated, then nodded, but went to a terra cotta jar with a dipper attached and swallowed some cold water first. When he sat down again he started to roll a cigarette but his fingers were bloody from the wound in the back of his head and she reached out impulsively, took the makings from him and built him a smoke. He nodded his thanks as he got a match out and lit up.

'Not the first one you've made.'

'I used to roll them for my father. He had bad rheumatics and his fingers were all crippled. Then, when Wayne started smoking, I taught him how and—' She stopped abruptly, coming back from her distracting nostalgia. Her voice was sharp when she said: 'Get on with your story!'

He blew smoke and nodded, sitting in the only other chair, obviously getting things straight in his mind. He noticed the rifle barrel still pointed at him across the small table.

'From what I've seen of this neck of the woods, mostly in half- or full dark, it must've been somewhere over the other side of this mountain where I came across this wounded feller—'

'At last we get to it!' she gritted, her tone of voice surprising him. '*Now*! No more delays! Tell me what happened, starting with the man's description.'

'Gimme a minute to think. . . .' She stood up and whipped the rifle around, thumbing back the hammer again. He reared back in his chair, held out both hands. 'Judas priest! Will you take it easy? You were the one hit me with the rifle butt, loosened my brain. . . .'

Her mouth tightened and she sat down slowly, but did not lower the rifle's hammer. 'Get – on – with – it!'

He did, without any more delays.

CHAPTER 5

WAYNE

Chance Lawton knew that by now he should be closing in on his horses, but he had a notion that he was going to be too late to do much to recover them. . . .

This Captain Brodie Hall didn't ring exactly true. Sure, he was in the army, all right, Second-Seventh Cavalry, or something, but there was a certain raggedness and lack of discipline with his 'patrol' that was way too slack for an official mission.

No doubt they were looking for horses and tresspassers, but he figured that their main aim was to profit from whatever they found. He hadn't been all that surprised when they had jumped him, though he wondered why they had left him alive. Plumb laziness, an oversight, thought he was dying anyway. . . ? Didn't matter – he was alive. . . .

Now, in strange and rugged country, leaning on his

saddle horn, thinking about this, he suddenly realized he could see the body of a man lying on a small rise, barely visible through the shimmering heat haze. Sun glinted from a belt buckle, or maybe a gun, tilted half-out of its holster. He rode across, Colt in hand as he dismounted. Warily, he approached from above where the man lay, then saw the blood splashed on the ground, blotching the back of the blue shirt.

The man had dirt and blood smeared over his youngish face. Lawton figured he was in his twenties. He had a small pencil-line moustache, almost camou-flaged now by several days' stubble growth. A few inches short of six feet, he was wide in the shoulders, but he didn't seem all that fit; his flesh had a soft look and feel to it and his hands were without calluses. Lifting an eyelid, he saw the eye was blue, with gold flecks. . . .

'Oh, dear God! That – that's Wayne!' the girl exclaimed, star-tling him, stopping his next word, briefly, her hand rising to her mouth in the dimly lit mountain cabin.

Lawton merely looked at her, held up a hand to stall off a major interruption, then continued his story. .

The chest wound was high up: the bullet seemed to have missed the lungs and other vital organs. But he was breathing with some difficulty. Then Lawton noticed the back wound, too; the bullet was bulging under the skin after having skidded across the ribs. He cut it out and the man moaned, thrashed weakly and swore once, only half-conscious.

Chance didn't bother about the scalp crease, except to wash it with water; it was not a serious wound. He had lost a lot of blood, though; was still bleeding.

There wasn't much in McCracken's saddle-bags he could use for first aid, but by tying together a couple of bandannas and a kerchief he made a rough bandage. It might not do much to stop the bleeding, but it was the best he could manage with what he had. He slid the man's bloody, bullet-torn blue shirt on him to help hold the bandage and pads in place. He rigged a temporary shelter by propping up the saddle on one end and tenting the saddlecloth over the man; it shaded his head and upper body and he at last responded to the sips of canteen water, rolled those strange, gold-flecked eyes towards his mentor.

'Th-thanks.'

'You got a name?'

'W-W-Wa . . .' The word faded down into his heaving chest so that Chance wasn't sure if the man said 'Wade' or 'Wayne' or something else beginning with 'W'. He settled on 'Wade'. He told the man his name, adding, 'What happened?'

The wounded man took quite some time to answer, told his story in snatches of a few words, or just a single addition. Some of it was obviously out of sequence but, eventually, giving him frequent sips from the canteen, Lawton worked it out this way:

Wade Whoever-he-was, was an ambitious young journalist working for one of the well-known mid-west newspapers, the *Denver Sentinel*, which also produced a bi-monthly magazine called *On Watch!* This had started out merely as a rehash of current news with added hindsight comments, but a few word-sketches about pioneering types, occasionally accompanied by a drawing, unexpectedly proved to be very popular. So they added interviews with real frontier lawmen and adventurers. When a new editor took over the style became more serious and socially oriented, the magazine began dealing with topical issues, preferably controversial and with political overtones that got under the skin of the readers – like the proposal to limit the size and number of new paddle-wheelers on the Big River System; banning on-river gambling within a mile, approach or departure, of the towns; the use of public monies – unofficially but widely known to finance young, attractive 'ladies' for the onboard 'comfort' of gentlemen travellers: *On Watch!* even named some politicians who used such services.

The *Watch,* as most folk referred to it now, began to earn a name for itself by exposing graft and corruption. Circulation grew at an astounding rate. The editor was honoured by his peers for his courage in his crusading work. Big Eastern papers began to show interest, publishing his editorials; two Boston publications even bought shares in the *Sentinel,* the parent paper.

One of them was openly 'agin the government' in Washington, publishing its often inflammatory and defamatory tirades under what they termed 'Freedom of the Press'. It was suggested that anything that would harass the current party in power would be regarded as immediately acceptable and the reporter behind any exposé, substantiated or not, would be richly rewarded – not only monetarily but with a high position in the growing magazine empire.

Wade saw it as his big chance, met with a man named Ballantine who had recently returned from the Black Hills of Dakota and who claimed he had made his fortune there in gold, which the government denied existed in the area. He had been warned to keep quiet about it, in fact, he had been mysteriously beaten up badly enough for a stay in hospital, where Wayne Daniels found him. Being an old Princeton man, like Wade (or Wayne), he told him his story.

Wade set off to run it down, especially the part where Ballantine claimed he had seen dozens of Indians; Lakotas, Dakotas, and others, enslaved by avaricious whites wearing ragged army uniforms, forcing the Indians to work under their guns or the threat of harm to their families.

To his surprise, by following Ballantine's directions, Wade/Wayne discovered the location of the mines, but was himself flushed out and had to make a run for it. He was pursued, shot off his horse above a river, and both he and his animal plunged into the raging currents. The horse was jammed brokenly between two large protruding rocks, the frothing water tinged red; Wade's legs swayed in the fast current from behind another rock some yards downstream.

'L-left me for – dead,' Wade/Wayne gasped, fingers clutching convulsively at Lawton's hand. 'I-I don't remember how I got out of the – river or here. H-help me find – a town with a – telegraph – must get – story in. Nothing in writing – all up here. . . .' He tapped his head and winced. 'Must – send it – through. Will you—?'

Lawton told the man he would do his best and, scouting around, found a small cave that would be ideal for the night. They turned in, Lawton near-exhausted from long days of hard riding behind him to this place, and caring and manhandling this wounded man, who weighed at least 180 pounds.

Lawton, his voice a little hoarse now, took another dipperful of water and looked across the table at the girl in the half-gloom of McCracken's mountain cabin.

She was breathing fast. 'Did you reach a telegraph station?' she asked anxiously.

Lawton hesitated, shook his head slightly. 'No. Wayne disappeared from the cave during the night,' he told her flatly. 'Dunno whether he just wandered off, or was fully conscious and knew what he was doing. Or maybe he felt afraid of me, after telling me his story. I tried to track him but lost his trail above a big waterfall. I climbed down and spent all morning searching the banks, and the shallows amongst the rocks, too, but couldn't find any sign of him. I'm sorry, ma'am, but I decided he hadn't made it, that the fall had killed him.'

'So you just went about your own business!'

He looked at her sharply, but he could savvy her accusing tone. 'I was taking too long to find Brodie Hall or my horses. I'd been told he'd already gotten rid of them, but I wanted to be sure there was nothing else I could do.' He glanced levelly at her pale, taut face. 'I'd done all I could for Wayne.'

He left it at that; if she couldn't see that – well, too bad.

But she sighed, and wiped glistening tears from her eyes. 'I – thank you for helping Wayne as much as you did. It's ironic – he was a very keen newspaperman, always looking for a story that would be a "smash" as he called it; it seems he found one – and – and died before he could write it.'

Lawton felt uneasy though he was careful to keep his face without expression. He felt sorry for this girl, though knew nothing about her.

Then, suddenly, her pale face turned towards him, the angle of the light making her high cheekbones more prominent. She half-rose out of her chair, exclaiming: 'But he's not dead! He can't be!' She waved the bloody shirt at him.

Chance looked at her sharply. 'You're right! How else could his shirt have gotten here? Somehow he must've survived the waterfall, or maybe he didn't even go over the edge. The tracks were pretty muddled and there was just no sign of him anywhere I looked. But he must've made it across the range, saw this cabin and. . . .'

The hope flared on her face and he cursed himself for raising such an emotion in her, even though what he said was true. It was just possible Wayne Daniels was still alive and wandering around these mountains, but. . . ?

She seemed deep in thought, which process he decided not to interrupt, half-afraid to hear what she was mulling over. Then Abby Daniels said quietly,

'I wonder—? If I paid you, would you – help me look for Wayne, Mr Lawton?'

He was shaking his head before she had finished.

'Can't do it, ma'am. I've come to terms with the fact I've likely lost the horses, but I still have to find Abe McCracken. He murdered an Indian friend of mine and no law court will ever punish him, not with the backing Captain Brodie Hall and his men will give him. Besides, he stole my mount, and a Mexican saddle that I'm mighty attached to.'

At first she looked mildly puzzled, then seemed shocked. 'You mean . . . *you*'ll see your friend is avenged?'

'No one else can, and I sure don't aim to let McCracken get away with the killing. He just yelled "*He's trying to escape!*" and shot him dead. And Brodie Hall will back him all the way. So, it'll have to be rough justice. Mine.'

Her expression tightened in the face of such cold determination, but then brightened slightly. 'But if you are looking in this general area . . . couldn't we . . . combine our "interests"?'

'Aw, no, Miss Daniels. Look, I can't say your brother would survive his wounds, but he's young and tough and I figure he has a pretty good chance. But no, I'm sorry. I've got this lead on McCracken now and—'

'The lead brought you here, but McCracken's gone.'

'Yeah, but an oldster gave me an alternative place to look. It's dangerous and he could be with outlaw friends. In other words, there's likely to be gunplay and someone's going to get killed.'

'It's good of you to think about my safety, Mr Lawton. That's what you're doing, isn't it? But after our parents died in a stampede I had to rear my young brother. I love Wayne very much and I'll risk anything to help him. I can take care of myself. I run a large ranch in Wyoming, horses *and* cattle, and I have a dozen hardbitten men in my crew. I assure you not all of them are gentlemen and they take a good deal of controlling. I'm not boasting when I say that now they do what I tell them without much argument. After I shot one who tried to break into my bedroom. . . .' She let her voice trail off and he pursed his lips. 'And I'm the outdoors type. I love working on the open range, camp out whenever I can, hunt my own food. I won't be a burden, Mr Lawton. Not to you, nor any man.'

She seemed amused at his changing expression as many and varied thoughts raced through his head. At last he cleared his throat and said. 'We – I'll have to cross to the other side of the mountain. . . .'

She smiled faintly. 'Mr Lawton, I think – I think you want to help me. You surely must see how it makes sense for us to combine our efforts. Why're you fighting it?'

He wondered himself.

'I'm not short of money. I can pay you well.'

Damn! He knew he was going to give in, but he just

didn't want to say so. He didn't even know why he was being so cantankerous.

'It's still too risky. McCracken's a killer. And any of his pards he joins up with are bound to be the same.'

'But I'll have you to protect me.'

'Ah, hell!' he said, spreading his hands. 'You don't give a man much room for argument, do you?'

'There's no need.'

She smiled widely for the first time and it was as if someone had turned up the lantern. Hell almighty! What was wrong with him, thinking that way?

'Aah!' he growled. 'I'm not used to handling women.'

She kept the smile, and her eyes looked mischievous. 'You won't exactly be "handling" me. . . .'

'Dammit! That's what I mean! I say something and it's clear enough in my mind, but you – women – can turn it around to make it mean somethin' else!'

She saw how agitated he was becoming, but something told her he would be as cool – and as hard – as a rock in the bottom of a mountain stream in any real life-threatening situation, especially if guns were involved.

Though still amused, she made herself look contrite.

'I'm sorry, Mr Lawton, I didn't mean to. . . .'

'Might as well call me "Chance",' he said in resignation and rather grumpily, 'if we're gonna be pardners.'

She fought to hold back the smile that wanted to stretch her lips.

'Thank you. I'm Abby as you know, and I'll be happy to take my "chance"!'

Her half-smothered laughter covered his groan.

He'd like a dollar for every time he'd heard *that!*

CHAPTER 6

DANGEROUS HILLS

'*Both* dead! Landers *and* Willis?'

Jude Hall couldn't believe it as Top-Sergeant Simms fought his sweating horse to a standstill. Wearily he dismounted by the campfire the four-man posse had built within a ring of boulders, which shielded it effectively.

Simms was a tough-looking cavalryman of eleven years' experience. He had spent part of that time in the stockade at Fort Whipple but it had done little to improve his brutal ways. It had been the best thing he'd ever done, joining up with Brodie Hall and his wild bunch of ex-soldiers, who still masqueraded as genuine soldiers when the occasion called for it.

'They both died hard by the looks of it. Landers went off a cliff, weighed down with lead. Willis had most of his head missin'.'

Jude Hall swore. 'Knew that damn 'breed was a

passel of trouble, soon's I laid eyes on him.' He kicked over the almost empty coffee pot, just as Simms was reaching for it, a battered tin mug in one hand.

'Hey! I was just gonna pour myself a cup!'

Jude glared. 'Brew up some more, Top, or curl up and die of thirst. Makes no difference to me.'

Simms swallowed the retort that formed in his outraged brain; he knew that look on Jude Hall's face. The man was mad enough to kill and wouldn't worry about the consequences, all because this Lawton had got the better of him in the livery. He tossed the mug aside and sat down beside the other three men, started to roll a cigarette. None of them said anything, their hard faces devoid of expression.

They were not the kind to show any compassion for Top-Sergeant Simms, or anyone else.

'All right. Put out the fire and let's move.'

Their heads all snapped up and startled gazes shot in Jude Hall's direction.

'Christ, Jude! It's pitch black!' The man who spoke was called Skag, blocky as a beer barrel and with legs like tree trunks.

'Fancy you noticin' that!' the sheriff snapped, throwing his saddle blanket on his mount. 'And what the hell difference does it make?'

'Well, for one thing it'll be damn hard to do any trackin'. . . .'

'And we might ride into a headshot in the dark!' said the man next to Simms, Mort Reece.

'Have to have eyes like a cat to even try for a headshot in the dark,' allowed the fourth posse man, Barrett.

Jude Hall grunted. 'We know he'll be tryin' for the Post. We'll make our way straight there. We know this country better'n Lawton. We'll cut up through that big dry wash under Drunk Man Butte; might even get there ahead of him. . . .'

They grumbled but Jude had the authority, and they all knew big brother Brodie would expect them to obey him.

No one, not even the Good Lord himself, would care to argue with Cap'n Brodie Hall when he was well and truly riled.

It wasn't for nothing that the townsfolk called the family – behind closed doors and in whispers, natu- rally – 'The Halls From Hell'.

'Hurry it up, Goddamnit!' snapped Jude, tighten- ing his cinchstrap.

'We gonna take time to bury Landers and Willis?' Skag asked.

Jude glared over his horse. 'Not unless you wanna keep 'em company – stretched out right alongside 'em.'

That ended any more discussion before they mounted and rode away into the night, all cursing Chance Lawton for bringing this upon them.

The girl watched Lawton dusting of his trousers before remounting his buckskin. As he settled into leather she said,

'Are you sure you aren't part Indian?' Even in the dim light she caught the puzzlement in his eyes. 'I mean – look how dark it is, yet you find what you call "sign". Indians are supposed to have that ability but I've never met a white man who could track in the dark with any accuracy, and you've been right twice already.'

'Just using logic. Figure the general bearing we want and, with the stars and the position of the moon, I just look for something out of the ordinary along what I figure is the direction we need to go.'

'Is that the Indian way?'

'Could be. I dunno.' He briefly told her of his past as he knew it: found naked in the wasteland, no white settlers for many miles around and even then no one knew him. 'Could be I'd wandered off from some Indian camp. But I was mostly reared by whites, mighty good folk. I've spent a lot of time with the Sioux, so I guess I do have a kind of affinity with Indians.'

She smiled. 'More like "compassion".' Again that puzzled look on the blur of his face. 'You *are* a compassionate man, Chance Lawton, even if you don't realize it, or don't want to acknowldge it.'

'You don't know me well enough to say that,' he told her curtly. He lifted his left arm and pointed. 'Up slope and round the base of that leaning butte. That's the way.'

He touched his spurs to the buckskin's flanks and she followed, wondering why she had placed so much trust in this man; as he had said, she hardly knew him.

The trail became much more difficult once they'd rounded Drunk Man Butte. It ascended and they had to dismount and lead their reluctant horses, tugging hard on the reins in some places; once, Lawton almost had to lie down as he put tension on the buckskin's reins. Its reluctance communicated itself to Abby Daniels' bay, but Lawton eased up, patted the buckskin's head while speaking to it softly, coaxing, reassuring the quivering animal, *calming* it before her eyes.

It was still reluctant but didn't fight so hard and, once it began moving, Abby's bay followed.

'That's said to be another Indian trait: whispering to a horse like that, somehow making it understand.'

He gave her a crooked smile. 'Was taught to me by a white man; best bronc-buster I ever met.'

'Oh, I give up! I'm just grateful that I met you, otherwise I wouldn't have any hope at all of finding Wayne.'

He said nothing, but had one brief thought: *If we find him, in these hills, it'll be a miracle.*

They covered more ground faster than Lawton had figured, the slope still rising, but with undulations and even short stretches of flat ground running across the grade.

They stopped to let the horses rest – and themselves, for they were still afoot. Soon after they started again, they rounded the side of the butte and it rose sheer above them, but the base angled down and even Abby could make out the narrow zigzag of a descending trail.

She was excited as they mounted again and started off. But her tension came back when she saw him unsheath the rifle and check it before laying it across his thighs.

71

'Why? Is there something you aren't telling me?'

He hesitated. 'Thought I saw something move down there.' He pointed but it was towards a dark patch of moon shadow that her eyes couldn't penetrate.

'How could you see?' she asked before she could stop herself.

He didn't answer but after descending a few more feet said, 'Might've been an animal.'

She felt herself tense; riding her home range she had faced wild animals of all types, but only once alone; it had been a big cat of some kind, dropping silently off a ledge, actually knocking her out of the saddle as it locked claws and fangs into the neck of her mount.

She had managed to kill it with her six-shooter but it was too late for the horse and she had to walk five miles back to round-up camp through country that she knew was crawling with predators. She only had three shots left in her six-gun; she fired two, keeping the last one. . . .

But it had been enough; two of her riders had found her just on daylight. It was the last time she rode the range without a carbine and spare ammunition.

Now the fleeting memory of that time sent a cold wave through her. But almost immediately she began to relax.

She didn't really know why, but she felt . . . safe with this strange, taciturn man riding a few yards in front.

They passed close to the place where he thought he

72

had seen movement without incident; but just in case he had seen danger, she now carried her carbine across her thighs, her hand sweating against the wood and cold metal. The trail took a dip, then rose steeply, and it was while they were fighting their mounts up this part, the animals scrabbling for a foothold, that a man appeared on a rock beside them.

There was enough light left in the sliver of moon to gleam from the rifle he held.

'Cocked and locked, feller. Just let your rifle slide off your lap and grab a couple of handfuls of air!'

Lawton swore softly; he had been looking down, trying to pick out some solid ground for the buckskin, and had missed seeing the guard. There was no choice now; he let his Winchester slide off into some brush and the guard instinctively watched it fall.

The man's big mistake had been giving Lawton all his attention: he hadn't even noticed the girl's carbine held across her lap. Now, without thought she swung it up and, hesitating for the space of a sharply indrawn breath, moved the barrel a hair so she wouldn't shoot Lawton, and squeezed the trigger.

Lawton went out of the saddle like a log leaving the down-end of a water-chute, the closeness of her bullet causing him to react by pure instinct: self-preservation at any cost. The slug ricocheted from the rock beside the guard. He staggered as chips flicked ixito his face. He missed his footing and slid off his rock, down on to the trail where Lawton was already bouncing to his feet.

The mustanger lunged forward and kicked the rifle

from the man's hand. The guard grunted, spun away and grabbed for his six-gun, but Lawton charged in, head lowered, got his arms about the man and lifted him completely off the ground, hurling him down slope. As the guard floundered, Chance went after him, long-striding, arms flailing so as to keep his balance. As the man rolled on to his back, six-gun now in hand, the mustanger jumped.

He landed with both boots on the man's gun arm. The guard screamed in pain, then Lawton fisted-up the front of the man's shirt, jerked him half-erect and hammered three violent blows into his face. The man collapsed and Lawton kicked him away so that his body slid down another six feet, raising a cloud of dust. He clawed his way back up to where the girl waited.

'Come on! That shot'll bring whoever he was guarding . . . Goddammit!' He rapped this last as he tried to locate his rifle, spun as he thought he heard a horse upslope and lunged for the buckskin which was stomping a little.

He leapt into the saddle and almost rammed into the girl's bay as he cut across the slope. The buckskin was gathering speed when he heard her cry out; he twisted in time to see her horse going down, where it had put a foot wrong.

He fought the buckskin around, and slithering and sliding, made his way back to where she was clambering up, trying to reach the staggering bay. Lawton wrenched the reins, got the buckskin slightly above the other horse, then came down. He leaned far out from his saddle, reaching for the bay's flying reins. His fingers closed over the leather and he was almost yanked right out of the saddle as the bay tossed its head, momentarily fighting the drag on the reins. By the time it realized it was being steadied, the girl had clawed her way up, grabbed a stirrup and slid her small foot into the oxbow.

She was just settling into leather when four horsemen rode out of the night, all with guns drawn.

'Told you we'd meet again, 'breed, you son of a bitch!' Jude Hall followed the curse with a harsh laugh. 'Bring him here.'

'We get the gal to play with?' asked Top-Sergeant Simms hopefully.

'Not till I say so.' Jude sat his horse easily, holding his rifle with the butt on his right thigh, looking down at the struggling Lawton as Skag and Barrett dragged him across. Jude smiled crookedly and moved the rifle to both hands. Looking up, Lawton tensed, waiting for the brass curve of the butt to smash into his head. But Hall sneered, cursed again, and kicked Lawton in the temple. His legs folded and Skag caught him. His head lolled loosely on his neck as Abby cried out in protest.

'Leave him alone!'

Jude ignored her and motioned to Skag and Barrett. 'Tie him in his saddle and let's get on. Handy will've heard the shootin' earlier so don't go pot-shottin' at the first shadow you see. It'll likely be his men watchin' for us.'

'We goin' to Handy's camp?' asked Barrett; there

was a note of excitement creeping into his voice. He cut loose with a toned-down Rebel yell as Jude nodded curtly. His eyes were sparkling as he looked at the girl and said, 'Long Bob makes the best moonshine this side of Cheyenne!'

Simms and Skag showed interest. Lawton was semi-conscious as they roped him into his saddle on the buckskin.

Jude was sitting beside Abby, holding his rifle on her, casually. 'Dunno who you are, sweetmeat, but I've a notion you're gonna be sorry you ever come out here with Lawton.'

Barrett let loose with another Rebel yell. '*I* ain't sorry she come! An' I'll guarantee you that!'

Abby Daniels said nothing, but she felt the blood drain from her face and felt as if she might fall off her bay if she didn't tighten her grip on the saddle horn.

She drew down a deep breath and prepared herself to meet the nightmare she knew was waiting for her.

CHAPTER 7

BOOTS, SADDLES AND BULLETS

Chance Lawton had heard of Long Bob Handy, as most folk had in these northern United States, but he had never met the man. Till now.

And he wished he hadn't.

Handy was tall and straight, lean and tough as a sapling oak. He must be six-feet five or six if he was an inch, Lawton decided, as he watched the man draw on a pair of sweat-and-work-hardened leather gloves. They were so stiff and tough that the fingers might have been made of metal, the way they stuck out of their own accord. As Handy closed a fist, Lawton heard the leather creak and knew the motion required some effort even for the tall man.

He was about forty, scarred on the left side of his face, the narrow, straight slash that ran from temple to jawline suggesting it was from a knife blade. There was a big gap in his front teeth: two missing on top, three at the bottom. He was able to spit a stream quite accurately almost five feet through this gap.

He had demonstrated it earlier, for the doubting Abby, and had actually knocked a bluebottle fly down in mid-flight. She felt apprehensive at the way he was looking at her now. He jerked his bullet head, with its cropped steel-grey hair stubble in Lawton's direction. 'He mean anythin' to you?'

She didn't answer and he shrugged, suddenly spun and his gloved fists smashed into Chance Lawton's body, the thuds slamming like a meat axe into a half-frozen side of beef. Lawton was tied to a tree and sagged over on the ropes. They cut deep into his aching midriff as he retched drily.

'For God's sake!' Abby exclaimed, her face white as a tombstone. 'What d'you want from us?'

'You . . . well, we'll get around to that soon enough. You can amuse yourself by imaginin' what my men might have in mind for you. Ain't been a woman in this camp for nigh on a month.' He waved his thick eyebrows but didn't smile.

She felt her knees weaken and the men holding her, Skag and Barrett, grinned as they tightened their grips on her arms. Morton Reece ran a lascivious tongue around his lips.

Lawton remained still and silent – it was pointless to try to struggle against his bonds.

Jude Hall's posse had brought them here to Handy's hideout after linking up with McCracken.

There was no sign of Lonnie Bean, the man old Cass had said would warn McCracken. He had probably returned to the Post with whatever reward McCracken had given him. But it was apparent that Lawton had been set up: steered in the direction he said he wanted to go, but it was where *they* wanted him to go, and where they were waiting for him. It was the girl's bad luck to be with him.

Now it was time to pay the piper, but he wasn't yet sure that Long Bob Handy had been taken into the full confidence of Jude and Abe McCracken.

Maybe he could use that knowledge – later.

Then McCracken stepped into the firelight, chewing on some kind of red meat, gnawing it off a cluster of bones which he now tossed aside. He spat and used a greasy fingernail to lever a sliver of the tough meat from between his teeth. Watching the girl, he turned to Handy.

'Dunno who she is. But I doubt she knows anythin'. There was no sign of her when I left the cap'n.'

'I figure she came to meet Lawton,' said Jude Hall.

'I was searching for my brother—' started Abby, but Handy motioned her to be quiet and turned to Lawton, who was struggling to clear his head. It obviously hurt him to breathe. Handy spoke, still staring at Chance.

'Missy, you might not be in this, whatever the hell it is, 'cause I ain't been told yet why we got all these vis'tors. But you'll come in useful to my men. You know what I mean? But Abe there'll tell us a story first, just what this is all about, won't you, Abe?' The inference was that McCracken had *better* explain. 'Way everyone converged on this camp I figure I might's well nail up signs pointin' right to it. Now, you make yourself comfortable, but where I can see your face.'

'Cap'n sent us, Bob,' McCracken said, sounding confident. 'He wants you and your men in on this deal.'

'Hell, we're in, whether the cap'n wants us or not,' growled Handy, looking the girl over in a way that made her blush.

Lawton struggled to straighten against his tree.

'Leave her go, Handy. She knows nothing. She's looking for her brother, like she said. He's lost in these hills. She offered me a hundred bucks to help find him. Happens I was looking for McCracken, anyway.' He paused briefly, added with a touch of slyness, 'She don't know anything about the gold.'

There was a sudden silence amongst the rough men gathered around the big fire. They all set their gazes on Lawton. McCracken looked like he wanted to kill the mustanger right then and there.

Long Bob Handy slowly turned his gaze towards McCracken, then Jude Hall. 'Now ain't *that* interestin'?'

Lawton, despite his pain, grinned, blood trickling over his chin; it looked like it would be easy to set a cat among the pigeons here. 'They never told you, did they, Bob? Oooohhh my! Why don't you ask McCracken and Jude if they know anything about some Indian gold?'

Handy backhanded Lawton. It was a brutal blow,

but casually delivered, just something Handy figured he ought to do. All the time he kept looking at McCracken and Jude.

'I don't hear nobody tellin' me anythin'!' His eyes looked weird in the flickering light, seeming to flash, like distant gunfire at night, then flare wide. 'But someone better! You got somethin' to say to Ol' Long Bob, Jude?'

'Well, I – was gonna get round to it, Bob. I just—'

'He dunno all of it.' McCracken spoke up, getting all the attention now. 'He din' come into it till Brodie sent for him.'

'Then you're elected to deliver the sermon, Abe – and there better not be any more delays!' Handy twisted one hard glove into the palm of the other, the hard leather scraping loudly in the sudden quiet, only broken by the crackling of the fire or a sudden eruption of sparks as a twig burned through.

Abby Daniels stood stiffly, a slight frown on her dirt-smeared face, watching Lawton as he sagged awkwardly in his ropes. 'Come on, McCracken!' Chance taunted. 'Speak up! Tell 'em how you took a shine to my Indian saddle blanket, and my Mexican saddle, then decided you might's well take my sorrel gelding as well. Tell 'em what happened when you finally got to Cheyenne Crossing – and why the cap'n sent you into these hills. He knew I was after you, and made sure I followed a trail that'd lead me to you. And you were waiting. But Jude got to me first. Put your nose outta joint.'

McCracken's face was burning with pure hatred as

81

he glared at Lawton, who continued his quiet taunting.

'How come you found it, Abe? Do some hard riding, bouncing around a lot, wondered why the sorrel started acting up? He'd get kind of ornery – jumpy – mebbe tried to take a bite outta your leg?'

'How the hell you know that!' demanded McCracken, genuinely puzzled.

The distressed Lawton still managed a crooked grin. 'You shoulda put that saddle blanket back on after you decided to keep it. I always kept it folded twice to make a cushion between saddle and horse, save his backbone. But you, being the kinda lazy cuss you are, you just threw the saddle across the sorrel's bare back, didn't you? Kept the blanket for your bedroll. Which meant there was no cushioning, and the saddle rubbed on the hide. . . .'

McCracken moved towards the tree, fists knotting. But Long Bob stepped in front of Lawton, holding up one gloved hand. McCracken stopped, anger giving way to wariness now, as a gloved finger pointed at him.

'I told you – no more goddam delays! So far you ain't hardly opened your mouth! That better change – right now!'

McCracken nodded swiftly, licking his lips, making a peace sign. 'OK, Bob. Just take 'er easy.' McCracken jerked a thumb at Lawton. 'This 'breed come down outta the hills, drivin' a bunch of half-broke mustangs. But they was just cover for him to get on down to a town or even as far as Fort Savage, where he told the cap'n he does business with Colonel Helm sometimes—'

'Move it along, damn you!' gritted Handy.

McCracken nodded quickly. 'After the cap'n nabbed him, I took a shine to his sorrel and ridin' rig. Lawton's right: the damn sorrel started actin' up after we done a slew of hard ridin'.' He stopped when the impatient Handy took a menacing step towards him, quickly added, 'Bob, I was fightin' that sorrel all the way, when suddenly it really started actin' up – stiff-legged buckin', whinnyin', took a bite at my leg – *twice*! Thought the damn jughead was gonna throw me. I dismounted an' hauled off the saddle to make sure there wasn't a burr or somethin' underneath.' He shook his head. 'There wasn't, but there was a lot of like little . . . knobs, poking through the wash-leather saddle-linin'.'

'Knobs?'

'Yeah, like there was gravel or somethin' inside the seat. I run my hand over 'em, an' one with a sharp edge cut through the linin'.' He paused, swallowed, raked his gaze around the expectant group watching, straining to catch his every word. 'It – it shone like – gold.' He paused for effect; no one said anything, but there was a lot of breath-holding. 'It *was* gold. The saddle was stuffed full of gold nuggets!' They goggled and he added lamely, 'No wonder it felt so blamed heavy! But bein' Mex-made an' them usin' an iron frame, mostly, I figured that was why. Later I found it was only a carved-wood frame. Was the gold made it heavy.'

Long Bob Handy turned slowly to Lawton. 'Looks like you take over the sermon, Reverend.'

Lawton glanced at Abby who was frowning, puzzled, no doubt wondering why he had mentioned the gold at all.

Then she realized he had done it as a diversion. Which told her something about Chance Lawton; this was another reason why he was hunting Abe McCracken, besides wanting to avenge his Indian friend, Ishna-Kobay. He wanted his gold back, yet he was willing to use it to divert attention from himself – and her! So was it that gold, as such, didn't mean a hell of a lot to the mustanger? *Money* didn't; at least that had been her impression when she was trying to hire him to help her find Wayne.

Now, she watched him as he turned his gaze to Handy. 'It's Black Hills gold.'

'Hell, I already figured that! Everyone knows it's there, but the damn army won't let no white man in to work it. So how come you had a saddleful?'

'Long story.'

'No it ain't! You just get straight to the point. Where'd you get the gold?'

'Indians. I've lived with 'em on and off for years. So happened I pulled a young buck out of the middle of a buffalo stampede we were caught up in. I shot a bull, stood up on the carcass with the buck, who was busted up some. Stampede never touched us, just tore on by, on each side.'

'I've heard of that,' McCracken said, with perhaps a touch of unwitting respect in the look he threw Chance Lawton now. 'But never seen it happen.'

'I guarantee it's an experience you don't forget.'

'Jesus, Lawton, if you don't get on. . . !'

'He was the son of a visiting chief. Hurt pretty bad but he pulled through. When I left to bring my mustangs down to sell, the old chief gave me the saddle – stuffed with gold nuggets.'

'Nuggets?' All heads swung towards Jude Hall as he exclaimed. 'I never knew they was *nuggets*! Brodie never mentioned that. Most Injun gold is still mixed in with the ore and has to be crushed and separated.'

McCracken nodded curtly. 'Yeah. But these were pure, good-sized nuggets. Cap'n Brodie realized right away we were on to somethin' big here. There was a couple thousand bucks' worth in the saddle, but it was so pure, Cap'n figured there had to be a helluva lot more where that come from. Jude was to be ready to jump Lawton when he showed at the Crossin'. He did, but he let the sonuver get away—'

'I never *let* him do nothin'!' the sheriff snapped, flushing. 'He – tricked me!'

'*Shut up*!' roared Handy, waving a gun around wildly. 'Where's the gold now?'

Jude's mouth and tone were bitter. 'My trustin' big brother, Cap'n Brodie Hall's got it! Who else? He's even lookin' at land down at the river forks, figurin' to build himself and that snooty wife of his a damn mansion there! While we—'

McCracken saw Handy's face and spoke quickly: 'Idea was to jump Lawton and make him take us to where he got the gold. But there'd be Injuns to take care of.'

Handy set his hard eyes on the lieutenant, mouth

smirking now. 'An' if you'd figured you could do it without me, you'd never've told me! Only Lawton spoke right up.' He bowed slightly. '*Gracias, amigo*!' he said sardonically. 'One I owe you.'

'Aw, we aimed to tell you, Bob, seein' as this is your bailiwick,' Jude said hastily. 'Gospel!'

'Sure, sure. Now you pick up the sermon from here, Reverend, and tell – us – what – we – want – to – know!'

Abby held her breath, seeing the stubborn look cross Lawton's battered face.

'Let the girl go first,' he said, surprising her and everyone else.

'Forget the goddamn girl.'

'*Let her go*!' Lawton shouted down Long Bob, his eyes bleak. 'She's not in this, only by accident. Long as you hold her, I tell you nothing.'

'You like to bet your life on that?'

'My life don't look like much right now, anyway.'

Jude Hall, still smarting from the way Lawton had got away, stepped forward and hit the mustanger in the midriff. He set his boots wide, shoulders hunching as he got ready to batter the helpless man. Abby was shouting and struggling, but Handy strolled forward, and casually gun-whipped Jude to the ground where he hunched on his knees, holding his head and moaning. Handy placed a boot against him and roughly kicked him on to his side. Ignoring the groaning sheriff, he turned to Lawton. 'You got guts, Lawton, but no brains. You taken a look at where you're at lately?'

86

'Just turn her loose, Handy,' Lawton said, short of breath from Jude's blow. 'She'll take days to find her way out of these hills. We can do a deal during that time.'

Handy was silent, briefly, then shook his head. 'No. We'll do it my way. I'll give you a break for puttin' me in the picture. So, you got all night to sweat things out – an' to think about *this*: We gonna have us a leetle party, kind of a celebration, in anticipation of you showin' us where all this gold is, see? Then come sunup. . . .' He leered at the white-faced Abby. 'We'll start talkin' a deal.'

'Goddamnit, Handy! Can't you turn her loose?' Lawton said, struggling futilely, sick to his stomach that he hadn't bluffed enough to get Abby her freedom.

Handy held up his gloved hands placatingly. 'Relax, No one's gonna touch her – till I say so.' He raked his deadly gaze around the murmuring, disappointed outlaws. '*No one*! But, come mornin, Reverend, I'm gonna ask you again about that gold. An' when I do, I'm gonna be hung over an' in one helluva lousy mood. I ain't a patient man at best of times, but I'll be standing right next to the gal, and if your answer ain't what I want to hear. . . .' He shrugged, giving that big tooth-gapped smile. 'Well, everyone's so eager for a piece of her, I might have to get 'em to draw straws. Know what I mean?'

Lawton's eyes were disconcertingly deadly. 'You better pray I don't get loose, Handy!'

Handy laughed. 'You do, I'll let you have first shot.

That's how worried I am about you gettin' loose. All right. Let's get things under way and remember, the gal's outta bounds. For tonight only.'

He didn't have to spell out the threat. The fear and apprehension showed clear through the resentment on the disappointed faces of the outlaws.

They know he's an animal from experience, thought Lawton. Not one of 'em'll be game to go near her – till Handy says so. . . . Then. . . !

The party was wilder and rowdier than a mountain-man *rendezvous*.

Lawton didn't know what they were drinking but it was mighty potent, took no time at all to fill their pickled brains with wriggling worms. There were brawls and one vicious knife-fight that left a man dead. They pushed his body into a sinkhole as the victor snatched another bottle and put it to his lips. Someone took a shot at it and hit it on the third try. Exploding glass and burning liquor ravaged the man's eyes and he ran off down the steep slope, screaming. No one went after him, but it was some time before the screaming and sobbing stopped. Fazed, drunken men sprawled all over the slopes. Surprisingly few threw glances towards the prisoners, unless they did it surreptitiously.

Lawton looked at the girl tied to a nearby tree and saw she was biting her lip. Her pale face was almost luminous in the dim light, the flickering of the fire barely reached this part of the camp.

'Pretty sure Handy's got 'em scared white,' Lawton

said in an attempt to ease Abby's concern. 'No one'll come near us without his say-so.'

'You can – guarantee that?' she asked breathlessly. 'I-I'm sorry, Chance. I'm very frightened.'

'Don't worry. Handy's got a right mean reputation. I reckon it'll keep his men in line.'

'That's what I am worrying about! He's got to pass out sometime, and then. . . ?'

'No, it won't happen that way.' Lawton tried to sound confident but he had heard of Bob Handy and his so-called 'party-tricks' for years now, felt his belly knot up as he watched Abby. 'They're scared of him.' And rightly so, he added under his breath.

Three times men came over and checked their ropes, one trying to steal a kiss from Abby. She bit his lip and the man slapped her. But the look on his face told Lawton he would keep out of Handy's way in case he had to explain how he came by his bloody mouth.

Handy himself swayed across once, checked Lawton's bonds, smiled crookedly at him, then turned when he was six feet from the tree and spat accurately on Chance's shirtfront. Handy staggered off, giving a Rebel yell.

But things died down just before the sky began to lighten in the east. Men snored where they lay after the rotgut had caught up with them, and they all finished up on their backs.

The fire burned down to a few dull coals.

Despite her misgivings and anxiety, and her uncomfortable position, the girl dozed. Lawton was glad to see it; she was going to have to face the prospect of a terrible day in a couple of hours. Either that, or he was going to have to tell Handy where the gold came from. And that would involve a lot more people having a very bad day.

Lawton dozed several times despite himself.

Suddenly he lifted his throbbing head, blinking, wondering what had wakened him this time.

There was no racket from the camp downslope now; a wolf howled, but a long, long way off. Then he stiffened against his tree.

Something was tugging at the ropes that held him and there was a strange sound he couldn't place.

Then he recognized it: the *ssss-ssssssing* sound of a blade sawing through rope. . . .

Even as he realized this he felt his bonds dropping away, one by one.

CHAPTER 8

GETAWAY

He couldn't stand.

Lawton had been tied to the tree for so long the circulation in his limbs had been cut off or seriously interrupted. As the severed ropes fell like dead snakes around his ankles, he collapsed at the base of the tree.

In moments, Abby Daniels was kneeling beside him, cradling his head on her bent leg, pushing his hair back from his pale, battered face.

'Chance!' She was obviously concerned for him but kept her voice down. 'Can you stand?'

He blinked, shook his head, trying to clear the cobwebs. 'Pins and needles in legs and arms now. Blood's starting to flow again.' He gasped. 'Gimme a few minutes and I'll be able to walk. How the hell did you get free?'

'I cut her loose – same as I did you.'

Lawton's head snapped up and around. He made

91

out a man in the shadow of the tree, frowning because he couldn't see the features clearly and the voice wasn't familiar.

'Who's that?' he asked the girl; she was close enough and it was light enough for him to see her smile.

'It's Wayne! He saw us captured and brought in here, waited his chance and then cut us free.'

Lawton's head was spinning; he savvied what the girl was saying, but couldn't figure out how it had happened. 'Where the hell you come from?' he asked Wayne hoarsely.

Wayne said: 'Time for explanations later. I have your Winchester. Took it from the bush where the sheriff made you throw it.'

Lawton stirred now, rubbing his thighs and calves briskly. 'We're gonna need more than one rifle. Haven't got horses, I suppose?'

'No. But I know where they tethered theirs. In a small arroyo, over there.'

As he pointed, Chance groaned. 'We'll have to go tippy-toe through all those snoring drunks to get there!'

'No. I'll show you a way around. It's longer but it's how I got up here.'

'How long you been out here?'

'Hours. Come on, Chance! See if you can walk.'

They helped him to his feet. He swayed and his legs still felt a little leaden but he was able to walk, though somewhat drunkenly. Wayne handed him the rifle silently. Chance hefted the weapon thoughtfully.

'Well, come on!' Wayne said impatiently and Abby urged him to move, too.

'You two go get the horses. Run off the outlaws' mounts. Come back this way and pick me up.'

'What're you going to do?' asked the girl in a hushed voice.

'Get some guns. We might get away from this camp but when those rannies come to, they'll round up their mounts sooner or later and come after us.'

Abby looked quickly at her brother.

'Afraid he's right, Sis. But it's too risky, going in among them. Any one of them could wake up.'

'Then I'll put him back to sleep.' Lawton straightened now, his legs feeling more secure. He smiled faintly and tapped the curved brass butt-plate of the Winchester.

'I still think it's dangerous.'

'Sure it is, Abby. But it'll be more dangerous if they come after us and all we've got is the rifle. Dunno how many shots are left in the magazine, but it's not full. No more talk. Move, and don't worry too much about noise, just get our mounts and scatter the rest.'

He was moving even as he spoke, back down the slope towards the camp where the bodies were scattered like the aftermath of a massacre. He stepped over a deadfall and looked back.

Abby and Wayne Daniels had already moved off into the brush. *Good.*

The first man he came to had been sick all down his front and was muttering in his sleep. He stank. Lawton rolled him on to his belly with the toe of his boot, eased the six-gun out of leather but didn't try to remove the gunbelt.

He went from man to man, crouching, moving silently as any Indian, robbing the unconscious men of tobacco and gunbelts. He even tugged the boots off a couple who were really deep in oblivion, threw them into the rocks. The more panic and disruption the better. He found Long Bob Handy curled up outside a bark lean-to, hugging an empty bottle. He was tempted to slam the rifle butt between the man's eyes, but he resisted and turned away, after taking the Colt from the holster. Handy grunted but didn't wake up.

Chance had intended to toss the gun into the rocks or brush but as he turned and drew back his arm, a slurred voice said,

'Hey! That Bob? Keepin' a jug to himself? Gimme – gimme! Need a – drink . . . bad. . . .'

'Here, pard. Catch.'

Lawton tossed Handy's six-gun and the swaying, half-awake drunk tried to catch it. But Lawton had put some force into the throw and it took the man in the midriff. Breath exploded from him and he sagged, then cut loose with a loud moaning yell.

Lawton swore softly, two men nearby stirred, one sitting up, the other rolling over and looking straight up at Chance. He snorted, then started to scramble up.

'Hey! Hey, wha—?'

Lawton slammed the rifle butt against his head and he collapsed, rolled downslope on top of another man. It was early daylight now and the men were slowly stirring. This one happened to be Mort Reece and he recognized Lawton. He thrust himself up, yelling.

'Jude! Skag! Lawton's loose!'

Chance wasn't expecting it, but Reece drew and fired his Colt in a reasonably fast co-ordinated move. The shot was wide but Lawton instantly dropped to one knee, let the gunbelts fall from his left hand and triggered the rifle. Reece was hurled back by the bullet. Then all hell broke loose.

Disoriented though they were by the rotgut they had consumed the night before, the outlaws were still ready to fight at the sound of gunfire in the camp; they lived on a knife-edge of fear and the instinct for self-preservation took over even through the terrible hangovers that must be racking them.

Lawton dived for the ground as their guns blazed, most of them wildly, but a few slugs kicked gravel not too far from his body. He worked the rifle's lever and got off four more shots before the magazine emptied. He'd nailed two men, scattered others. He rolled to his knees, a six-gun in each hand now, shooting wherever there was movement. He recognized no one, but all were enemies and so legitimate targets.

The men scattered, yelling at each other, cursing, shooting two of their own comrades in their panic, the booze still fogging their brains as they crawled and scampered and tried to run for cover.

After emptying the two guns he had taken from the befuddled outlaws, Lawton buckled on a bullet belt and Colt. He ducked as lead whipped past his face, dropped low and rolled, somersaulting. He came up to one knee, the Colt seeking a target. Handy was up now, swaying, shooting wildly from in front of the lean-to with a rifle.

Lawton triggered and Long Bob staggered, grabbing at his side. He stumbled back into the lean-to and a bullet parted Lawton's hair above his left ear. It clipped the ear itself and the burning sting made him stagger.

A quick glance around told Chance what he had feared: he was slap-bang in the midst of the awakening outlaws. He should have been content with taking guns only from the men on the edge of the group; now he was trapped, surrounded.

They were going to get him! So, this was the end of the line; well, he could take a few with him before they nailed him. Where was McCracken?

He threw himself behind a collapsed pile of firewood, hands shaking as he thumbed cartridges into the loading gate of the rifle. The men's heads were clearing now with the life-or-death action and he dropped flat as a dozen bullets whined off the woodpile, splinters humming.

Then he heard a wild Indian yell and – *did he imagine it? The ground seemed to tremble!*

He looked up quickly and saw a dozen or more wild-eyed, mane-flying horses charging through the camp, driven on by the yells and occasional gunshots of Wayne and Abby Daniels.

The outlaws had to run – and there was nowhere to go but downslope. Men staggered and stumbled, falling over rocks and each other in their hurry to get out of the way of the stampeding mounts. They were still too groggy for their wobbly legs to steady them on such a steep grade.

Wayne veered across, leading Lawton's mount. Chance leapt up, ran to it, threw himself into the saddle, still holding the rifle. Mounting this way, on the run, encumbered with the Winchester, was nothing to a man who earned his living by breaking in wild mustangs. In seconds he was settled in leather and the rifle was at his shoulder, thundering shot after shot, chasing the panicked outlaws down the steep slope, half of them now rolling and skidding and tumbling after falling, out of control, unable to stop.

He caught Abby's eye as she reined back and let the horses run. He grinned and shouted, 'Let's get outta here!'

By full daylight they were on a sandspit that jutted into the bend of a creek, watering the horses. Once done, they retreated into the tree line, dismounted, allowed the horses to crop the grass while they reloaded the guns. Lawton rolled a cigarette, offered the makings to Wayne, but the young journalist refused with a shake of his head. Abby had wet a bandanna and, back turned, standing in waist-high brush, she washed the sweat and grit from her throat and breasts, sponged her soiled blouse.

'You sure look heaps better than when you ducked out of that cave,' Lawton told Wayne.

Daniels was wearing a checked woollen shirt that

97

was one size too small. He told Lawton he had found it in McCracken's mountain cabin. He'd taken off his ragged, bloody blue shirt and put the other on.

'It's a bit tight but helps hold those pads you put over my wounds in place. They're still sore but I can manage. I don't recall if I thanked you, but I do now – heartily!'

Lawton looked at him steadily. 'Why'd you run out?'

Wayne spread his hands. 'Don't know. Have no memory of it. My head was hurting, so I likely had concussion. I came to properly out in the brush, wondering where I was and how I'd got there. It was just daylight and I saw you obviously searching on the knoll. I thought you might be one of the men who'd shot me in the first place so I lay doggo. After you'd gone I tried to find my way out of the hills. It was all coming back to me slowly, how I'd stumbled on that slave mine, been spotted and pursued. I was lost and don't remember how long or where I wandered. But I found my way to a ledge. I saw you and Abby jumped by those four men. My memory had come back by then, so I hung around, followed at a distance. Then, when I saw my chance after they'd drunk themselves practically comatose, I crept in and cut you both free.'

Lawton drew slowly on his cigarette. 'Which I guess squares us away nicely.'

Wayne smiled, the action making him look even younger. 'We aren't out of trouble yet, unless I miss my guess.'

'No-ooo. I winged Handy but he's probably in the

saddle leading his crew on the hunt for us. They'll have their horses again by now and they know this neck of the woods like their own names. And Bob Handy won't quit, not with the smell of gold in the air.'

The girl returned from her toilet attentions and combed her fingers through her hair, loosening a few leaves caught up in the abundant strands. 'Where are we going?'

'Out of these hills,' Lawton replied, but he saw the frown that immediately came to Wayne's dirt-smeared face. 'Unless you have other ideas?'

Wayne glanced at his sister, gave her a half-smile, then nodded. 'I'd like to take another look at that mine where they've enslaved the Indians.'

'Isn't that somewhat – foolish?' Abby asked sharply.

Wayne shrugged. 'Maybe, Sis, but I didn't get a chance to see very much before I was spotted. Oh, I could turn what I know into a good enough article but I'd rather be able to give more details, like how many soldiers I saw and—'

Lawton stiffened. 'Soldiers?'

'Yes, but I don't think they were the genuine article. The uniforms were old and dirty. They might've been in the army once, but I think they were just dressed up to help keep the Indians . . . subjugated. You know, make it look like this was all official army business.'

'Sounds like Capin Brodie Hall. His group don't have any right to wear uniforms; they've already been discharged and, I'd guess, not too honourably. They dress up to scare and rob anyone coming out of the

Black Hills with horses or anything else that's valuable.'

'Like when they "confiscated" your mustangs,' the girl said. Lawton nodded and asked Wayne,

'You think you can find the place again?'

Wayne nodded. 'I've been thinking about it as I was going over the country I crossed while they were chasing me. I was pretty scared and confused, but wandering around, I've seen distant ridges and mountains that I think I recognize. I don't say I could back-track, as such, but I think I could probably locate the mine, or, at least the area, again.'

'I've got some business in the Black Hills myself, but what about Abby?'

Wayne glanced at his sister, but before he could speak she said, 'What about me? I'm coming, of course. Now, don't argue, either of you. What will you do if I don't join you? Leave me to find my own way out? With Bob Handy and McCracken and the others still searching for us?'

Wayne frowned. 'Well – she's right, Chance.'

Lawton smiled crookedly. 'Yeah. And doesn't she know it!'

CHAPTER 9

CHANCE'S COUNTRY

Jude Hall was exhausted. Not from fighting or running after the stampeded horses, but from arguing with Long Bob Handy, hung-over, belligerent and feeling bloody.

The outlaw boss now declared he was taking over the whole deal. He sat stripped to the waist; one of his men, a young ranny calling himself Salty, was kneeling and trying to wash the blood away from where Lawton's bullet had torn across Handy's lower left ribs. There was a glimpse of white bone and Handy on more than one occasion paused in his argument with Jude Hall to suck down a sharp breath and then release it in a string of curses aimed at Salty.

'S-sorry, Bob. But you're jumpin' all over the place!'

Handy casually slapped the kid across the ear, hard

enough to send Salty sprawling. Taking no notice as the young outlaw staggered up, shaking his head, Handy lifted an arm, pointing at Jude.

'Cap'n Brodie sent you here to deal me in, right?'

'If you were interested, Bob, but he only meant for you to – to join us, add to the numbers. Not to take over.'

Handy spat spectacularly through his gapped teeth. 'Then it's about time Cap'n Brodie learned better. I do deals, but *I* run things.' He lifted an arm as Salty hesitantly asked him to, and waited impatiently as the kid wrapped around him a length of cloth torn from a grimy bedsheet.

'Come on, come on, hurry it up, for Chris'sakes!' Handy gritted. 'I'll bleed to death before you get it bandaged. Jude, this is how things stand: I'm in this deal, right at the top. I know now there's gold nuggets out there somewheres, for the takin'. An' I'm damn well *gonna* take 'em! With my men. Up to the cap'n whether he comes with me or not. He don't, then he's the same as Lawton: just another target.'

'Judas, Bob, I-I can't tell him that!'

'You better! 'Cause that's the way it's gonna be. You wanna gimme an argument now, and you won't have time to draw a second breath before I get someone started diggin' you a grave.'

Jude was white, actually shaking, and all churned up inside. But he took a risk and said, 'Aw, Bob, you're hurtin' because Lawton winged you. Settle down some, have a drink an' we'll palaver. We'll run down Lawton first, if you like.'

Jude Hall leapt back as a six-gun appeared in Handy's hand, hammer drawn back under the man's thumb. Salty was sitting on the ground where he had toppled as the outlaw boss made his draw, thrusting the kid aside.

'Jude, I never liked you much. Never liked any of you damn Halls. I think I'm gonna put a bullet in you and send you back to Brodie tied over your saddle.'

Jude backed off, both hands out in front as if he could push Handy away. 'Jesus, Bob! T-take it easy, huh? I – I'll go tell Brodie. I'll tell him – tell him it'll be best if he joins up with you – and lets you run things, 'cause you know these hills better'n him.'

'Better'n anyone!' snapped Handy and Jude slowly released his breath: Handy wasn't going to shoot him on the spot after all. 'Hey – an' I don't care whether Brodie joins us or not. I'll find Lawton and this time he'll lose his toes and fingers one at a time, till he tells me where he got them nuggets. After his fingers and toes, maybe his ears.' He smiled crookedly. 'Or, if I'm still in a digit-removin' mood, I reckon he'll see reason – or he *won't* be seein' a certain part of himself ever again.'

The slowly recovering, red-eyed outlaws laughed, as did Simms and Barrett. Even Jude dutifully raised a snicker.

But his legs felt weak and he could hardly swallow, his mouth was so dry. Then he said, 'Well, guess I better be goin'. I'll be back with the cap'n and his men soon's I can.'

'We comin' with you, Jude?' asked Top-Sergeant

Simms anxiously.

Jude glanced at Handy, then shook his head. 'No. You stay and give Bob a hand with whatever he wants. I'll travel faster alone.'

'Not if you stand around beatin' your gums,' Handy told him harshly, lifting his Colt.

Jude strode quickly towards his mount.

Abby and Wayne Daniels sat their horses in the shade of a grove of trees and stared unbelievingly at Chance Lawton. The mustanger on his buckskin, had one heel hooked over the saddle horn while he rolled a cigarette.

'You don't trust us?' said the girl incredulously. 'You don't *trust* us? My God, what does it take to convince you that we're here to help you?'

Wayne, face pale and drawn with the pain from his back wound still giving him trouble, held up a hand, spoke to his sister though looking at Lawton.

'Just a minute, Sis. I think maybe I see what Chance is getting at.'

'You do? Then you have more brains than I have!' Abby was snappy, obviously outraged by Lawton's attitude. 'We've all helped each other from the time we met. Now – now he wants us to stay here and twiddle our thumbs, while he rides off into the hills and visits his Indian friends! Because he doesn't want us to know where they are!' Her eyes blazed at Chance as he lit his cigarette. 'It's . . . downright insulting, Chance Lawton!'

He rubbed the burnt match between thumb and

finger before letting it fall to the ground, sighed. 'I ain't insulting you, Abby, nor Wayne. Look, the tribes I stay with from time to time are good people. They like peace, but they'll fight if they have to – and enjoy it.'

'We aren't going to fight them!' she snapped.

'No. But it was their chief, Redfoot, who gave me that gold. I had no idea they had access to any. It's not important to them, leastways, not the same way it is to us whites. Where they got it I don't know. And I don't want to know. I don't want anyone else to know. *Anyone*.'

She flicked her gaze to her brother. 'See? He doesn't trust us.'

'Let him finish, Sis.'

Lawton drew deeply on his cigarette. 'It'll be easier for me to cover my tracks than to try to cover those of all three of us. Handy and his crew have stayed free in these hills for years. He'll have top trackers and every one of his men is trigger happy. If he finds his way to the tribe, it'll be a slaughter. He's likely sent word to Brodie Hall already, and if *he* brings his men, the Indians won't stand a chance.'

She stared at him unwaveringly as she digested this. 'But – you're talking about leaving Wayne and me exposed to Handy and his men!'

He shook his head. 'I'll show you a place you can hide safely. I have to see Redfoot, warn him that Handy and Brodie Hall are looking for that gold. Once he knows that, he'll take precautions and Handy could find himself following a trail that'll take him deep into the hills and on to land belonging to a *really* hostile tribe. If I took you with me, you'd know where they are and—'

'And if we were caught by Handy we might talk!' Abby blew out her cheeks in anger. 'My God! You're a cold-blooded bastard deep down, aren't you?'

Chance's face remained impassive.

'Sis, he's saying these are his people. Can't you see that?'

She snapped her head up. 'But you said you aren't Indian.'

'Said I could have some Indian blood in me. When those pilgrims found me they took me for an Indian kid at first. Had a lot of trouble from other whites when they said they'd raise me. Some folk saw me as just one more red man they or their kids'd have to fight some day. OK, I feel a mighty strong draw to the tribe, and the old *shaman* – must be nigh on a hundred – tells me my mother was part Indian, part Mexican. He didn't know who my father was, except that he was a white man. But that doesn't matter. I live life on both levels, white and Indian. I owe folks on both sides.' His voice softened as he watched her face. 'It's not that I *don't* trust you, Abby. I *can't*. I have to be sure the tribe's safe. I'm *that* much Indian.'

He crushed out his half-smoked cigarette against the saddle horn. 'I know this part of the country from here; I've hunted broncs all through this section, and I can take you to a safe place to wait for me. Or, if you don't want to do that, I can just ride out and lose you within five minutes.'

Wayne quickly held up a hand. 'No need for that.'

Abby studied him. 'I was right, wasn't I? You are ruthless!'

'And even a true bastard,' he said as he lifted the bay's reins, ready to ride. 'Coming?'

'*And* stubborn!' Abby added.

Wayne glanced at his sister's set face, then said, 'Lead the way, Chance. We'll wait for your return.'

Lacy Hall didn't look like either of his brothers, Brodie and Jude. He was a lot younger for a start, and had grown up spoiled rotten by Mother Hall because he was the youngest of her brood and she was unable to have any more children. When she died she left him the house, which he promptly sold and ploughed the money into a law agency. He had inherited the Halls' lack of scruples and was the richest man of his age in The Crossing.

A sour man, Lacy eventually set himself up as unofficial judge of Cheyenne Crossing, and it was simple to turn a dollar in the direction of his bank account.

He worked in with big brother Brodie by forging army authorization papers: he had a stock of blanks, somehow acquired a long time ago, which gave Brodie and his ragged 'soldiers' the necessary cover and 'authority' to act in the Black Hills under army orders, providing no one looked too closely at the papers. As most of the men they dealt with couldn't read or write it was simple to 'order' them to keep an eye out for gold but report only to him, not to any other army patrols they might meet.

'We're under special orders from Washington,' he would tell them conspiratorily. It always worked: folk liked to think they were privy to such things because they were trusted. . . .

He stared up now across his desk at Brodie Hall, who was wearing his captain's uniform. Lacy scowled. 'Yet another foray so soon, Broderick?'

'That's right. And I'm getting tired of your arrogant attitude, Lacy. You're paid well. I don't trouble you for much. You rake in all the fines you impose and they go straight into your pocket, so don't think that you are in any way superior to me. You're just another crooked lawyer, whether you admit it or not.'

Lacy blinked, took off his rimless spectacles and furiously polished the oval lenses with a silk kerchief. He moved his lips and nostrils, causing his neatly trimmed moustache to dance a jig. It amused the captain, who sniggered, the sound making Lacy angrier.

'All right! But you had better not make so many "patrols" into the Black Hills. Word gets around about all the soldiers prowling that country and some day someone at Fort Savage is going to wonder how come there are so many, when so few authorities have been issued.'

Brodie sniffed, lit a cheroot. 'With any luck, this may be the last for a long time. Perhaps the last, period. Now hurry it up; my men are itching to go.'

'Already?'

'Yes. Jude brought me news. With some luck we'll locate the source of those gold nuggets quickly.'

'Speaking of which, I haven't received my share yet. . . .'

Brodie sighed, dug in his pocket and handed over a small wash-leather poke. 'There you are; five out of the twenty McCracken found.'

Lacy frowned. 'Only twenty hidden in a Mexican saddle?'

'Yes. I know I would've packed in more myself, but – well that's how many there were. It was just a token reward to Lawton, it seems.'

Lacy stared, not entirely convinced. In fact, he knew damned well his brother was lying. He swept the poke into his top desk drawer and reached for the army authorization form: *Number A7/BH South Dakota Territory.*

As he wrote, Brodie said casually, 'While I'm absent, find out just how much bounty is being offered for Long Bob Handy and his gang, will you?'

Lacy's pen stabbed the paper and ink blotched the painfully formed writing.

'Damn you, Broderick! Look what you've made me do!'

'Get a new form and start again,' the captain said off-handedly. 'And don't forget to find out the value of those bounties. We may make this the most profitable "patrol" of all, if we play our cards right.'

'If *you* do! I'll be sitting back here, well out of it – and glad of it!'

Lacy crumpled the form, tossed it into the waste-bucket, opened the drawer and took out a fresh one.

'Hurry it up a little, will you? The men will be

growing impatient.'

Lacy scowled and began to write in his beautiful copperplate hand.

When he reached the bottom line that said, *Issuing Officer*, he paused, right hand poised over the space, then scrawled quickly, in huge contrast to his copperplate.

The 'signature' was unreadable, except for the first word: *Colonel.*

CHAPTER 10

BLOODY HILLS

The canyon was teeming with wild horses. It was a large area, with a stream that meandered through a thick clump of trees, grassy slopes, and a couple of boulder-fields studded with rocks large enough for the mustangs to hide behind.

No doubt the big cats prowled the night shadows, hoping to bring down a newborn foal or a young colt, frisky but inexperienced in the ways of hungry predators.

'There're plenty of birds, wildlife in general, if you want to hunt for grub,' Lawton told the girl and her brother. 'But you shouldn't be here that long. If all goes well I'll meet Redfoot early afternoon. I'll come back soon as I can.'

'Does that mean after you've ridden deeper into the hills, searching for the slavers' mine?' Wayne looked anxious. 'I need to get more first-hand knowledge of what's going on in these hills, Chance. I think I should come with you.'

'And leave Abby alone?'

The girl frowned at her brother. 'You're more dedicated to that damn paper than I thought, little brother!'

The young journalist looked uncomfortable. 'I-I have a good reputation amongst the newspaper fraternity, Sis; I have to maintain it. And, believe me, this is a big story. Once it becomes public knowledge I'll really be on my way.'

Her face was sober, the eyes narrowed. 'And I thought Chance was selfish! But we're siblings, and you're talking about leaving me here with all those killers loose.'

'You heard Chance. It'll only be until this afternoon.'

'Enough,' snapped Lawton, throwing Wayne a cold look. 'You stay here and look after Abby. I'll see you get in on any raid once we locate the slavers' mine.'

'See? That's where I can help! I . . . think I can find my way back there—'

'Stay put, Wayne. Redfoot'll send out his scouts. We'll pinpoint the mine before moving in.'

The younger man almost pouted. 'I need to go on that raid! My whole future's at stake!'

'Not going to argue, Wayne. Stay right here and you'll be safe. I give you my word I'll come back for you and take you to the mine.'

Wayne obviously wasn't satisfied and his shoulders slumped. He nodded surlily, glared at Abby. 'It'd only be for a few damn hours!'

'Oh, go and be damned to you!' Abby snapped. 'I raised you, but I never thought you could be so mean.'

'I'm not, Sis! But I'll never have another chance at a story like this—'

He grunted suddenly and his legs folded under him. His eyes crossed as he took a single stumbling step forward and then collapsed in a heap.

Abby, mouth agape, watched Lawton put away the Colt he had used to slug her brother.

'Hope I didn't give him another concussion.'

'My God! You – you could've killed him!'

She dismounted swiftly and knelt beside her moaning brother. Lawton shook his head slowly, mounted the bay and started to ride away.

'You can't leave him like this!'

'You're there to look after him. Make sure he stays in this canyon. And you'd better get the horses out of sight in those trees.'

'I think my brother's welfare is more important than horses!'

'Have it your way. *Adios.*'

She jumped to her feet as he rode back towards the narrow entrance. She started to call after him, but stopped when Wayne moaned again. She took the canteen down from her horse and looked at Wayne, who was rolling his head from side to side now, beginning to mutter unintelligibly.

Lawton hadn't hit him very hard, after all. . . .

Sighing, she set down the canteen, gathered up her reins and those of the horse Wayne had been riding, and led both animals up the slope to the trees.

Lawton was right; they would be best kept out of sight.

But the delay because of Wayne's arguing had been long enough for Handy and his men to reach this part of the hills.

It was young Salty who spotted Chance Lawton on a high ledge, urging his bay up a steep part of the slope towards the crest of the ridge.

The mustanger was too busy fighting the mount over the rough terrain to notice the bunch of riders coming out of the woods far below. As soon as Salty pointed out Lawton, Handy urged the man back under cover.

'We can split up, Bob,' suggested a red-bearded outlaw called, of course, 'Red'. 'I'll take half around the base, you go after him and drive him right into our arms.'

'You won't fool Lawton that easy.' Handy stood in his stirrups, watching the high rider drawing closer to the crest. 'Anyway, McCracken's ridin' the lower trail – he'll likely spot Lawton. Wonder where the sonuver came from?'

Red was restless, as were some of the others now that one of their quarry was in sight. 'It don't matter where he's *been*, Bob! We can see him – and we can get him if we move fast.'

Handy held up a hand as Red and a couple of others started to lift their reins.

'We been followin' the tracks of three riders. Where's the other two?' Handy mused, then smiled crookedly. 'One of 'em must be whoever set 'em free, and the other just has to be the gal.'

His words got the attention of his men then.

'You mean – go after her?' Red was incredulous. 'Hell, she's a looker, Bob, but you could buy a dozen like her once we get that gold. . . .'

'And how's the easiest way of findin' it?' Handy demanded, jerking a thumb towards the crest of the ridge. 'With the girl we've got our ticket to the gold. Lawton won't let anythin' happen to her. He'll do just what we tell him.'

The men stirred: that sounded all right to them.

Except Red. 'But Lawton's gotta get his Injuns to show him where they got the nuggets, ain't he?'

Handy looked exasperated. 'So? 'Long as we've got the gal, we call the tune. Now scatter and start lookin' around for somewhere he could've stashed her while he goes lookin' for his blood brothers.' He spat a stream and caused a watching lizard on a rock to topple off in fright. 'And I mean *blood*!'

Abby Daniels, trembling with anger, tugged on her riding-gloves and said sharply to Wayne, as he mounted his horse after the third try, still a little groggy:

'It's ridiculous you trying to ride so soon.'

'It'd be ridiculous if I sat here twiddling my thumbs and missed out on a first-hand encounter with those slavers, Sis! I'm sorry. But I'm going.' He settled into leather and she noticed he swayed a little, snatched at the horn. His tone was softer as he said, 'You'll be all

115

right here for a few hours, Abby.'

'No, I won't. Because I'm coming with you.'

'Oh, for God's sake. . . !'

But that was as far as his protest went; she settled into her saddle and spurred back towards the canyon's difficult entrance-exit.

Swearing, not feeling as chipper as he tried to make out,Wayne spurred after her but didn't catch up until she had covered ten yards. Her horse stumbled or he might not have been close enough to lean out and grab her bridle, hauling the snorting mount to a halt. His own mount was stomping, slipping a little on the steep grade.

'Abby! Can't you show some sense?'

'Can't *you*?'

Both were glaring angrily at each other when a harsh voice said,

'Well, howdy, sweetmeat. Fancy meetin' you here! We been sweatin' our pants off tryin' to find your hideout. Now, here you are. You come lookin' for me! Hey, ain't that somethin, boys? Must've liked our hospitality earlier an' couldn't wait to get more of it.'

Both Abby and Wayne swallowed, feeling the blood drain from their faces as Long Bob Handy and his search party surrounded them.

Lawton allowed the bay to have a blow once he topped out on the ridge. There were big rocks and some brush growing from cracks that provided enough cover.

He felt like another cigarette but refrained; the

116

smell of tobacco carried a long way in this pristine wilderness and usually meant a white man was close by. He didn't want to have a few young bucks looking for scalps come barrelling in, shooting first and not even bothering to ask questions afterwards.

The horse was strong, but the climb had taken a deal out of it. Still, it was recovering quickly and Lawton gave it a drink out of his hat – just a mouthful – then set it moving on the long, zigzag descent. He could see the gleam of water down there, and he recalled from a previous visit that there was a string of waterholes in that area. The canteen was low, so he decided to refill it, let the bay have another short drink, then cross over into what army geological maps showed as *Indian Territory*, and marked: *Hostile.*

But he could be in Redfoot's land by skirting the waterholes an hour or two after high noon. That would be fine; he hadn't liked leaving the Daniels in that canyon, though he figured it was safe enough. Wayne's head was filled with journalistic glory, so he could be a problem. Abby – well she said she ran a ranch in Wyoming and seemed at ease with the outdoors. If she wasn't so feisty. . . .

The thing was, it wasn't wilderness savvy that counted here, it was staying out of the grip of someone like Bob Handy or Jude Hall and his pards. They. . . .

He hauled rein swiftly. There was a rider below, watering a horse at the smallest pool. He looked sort of familiar. Yeah, he'd seen him with Jude Hall, one of the so-called posse. Barrett? Garrett? Something like that. Well, if he was here there were bound to be others and—

'Take her easy, Lawton. Real easy.'

The words were backed up by the clash of a rifle lever working. Lawton hipped slowly in the saddle, narrowed his eyes as he recognized McCracken and another man he'd seen in Handy's hideout. Then a third rider came out of the brush slightly above him and he knew him, too, as one of Jude's men.

McCracken's rifle barrel jerked. 'Keep goin' down, but hold them reins up real pretty, almost under your chin, where I can see both hands.'

There was no choice: *No chance for Chance*, he thought bitterly, obeying McCracken's orders.

When they came to the waterhole the man who had deliberately shown himself watering his horse there stood beside his mount, but with a cocked pistol in his hand now. McCracken rode up alongside. He held the rifle in his right hand, flipped Chance's six-gun out of his holster, then made to ride around the bay to its other side.

Lawton twisted slowly to keep an eye on the lieutenant – but he was too late.

The rifle slammed him across the head, knocking his hat into the pool. He followed it, stunned, not quite out to it. The shock of hitting the water made him gasp and blink, as the pain roared through his head like an express train on a trestle bridge. Gasping and half-choked. he came up spluttering and spitting.

The four men were amused at his antics as his high-heeled riding-boots slipped several times on the smooth rock bottom, causing him to go under each time. He floundered up and McCracken spurred his horse into the waterhole, freed a boot from the stirrup and aimed a kick at Lawton's head.

He saw it coming, jerked back, and the boot skidded across his forehead, splitting the skin. Blood flowed, but before it could blind him, he grabbed McCracken's leg and heaved upwards.

The big man yelled and went out of the saddle to land with a splash in the shallows.

He staggered and stumbled in his efforts to get up. Chance waded towards him swiftly, clubbed a fist down into the big, coarse face, smashing the nose. Blood spurted. McCracken's knees gave way and he put down a hand quickly to keep from going under again. Lawton kicked the arm and the lieutenant went under. Lawton grabbed his shoulder, the shirt's material ripping as he did so. But he changed his grip and heaved the bloody-faced McCracken half-upright. He drew back his fist for a mauling blow, but it never landed.

Barrett rode in from the other side of the water-hole, and planted his boot between Lawton's shoulders, kicking him forward.

McCracken managed to get a foothold. He slugged Lawton with two savage blows, one from each fist. Chance's feet slid from under him and he splashed down, trying to keep his head above water. McCracken jumped up and landed on him with both feet, driving him under. Face bloody and wild-eyed, Abe McCracken pressed with all his weight, hands seeking

119

the back of Lawton's head, forcing his face down against the rock bottom.

Chance thrashed and kicked and bubbles burst up about his head, but he was effectively held under, drowning.

'Abe, *Abe*!' shouted Barrett.'We need him! He's got to show us the gold! Jesus Christ, man – ease up! Laredo, gimme a hand to get him off before he drowns the sonuver.'

It took the two men all their strength to break McCracken's grip. Lawton floated up, then coughed as he struggled to get his face uppermost. He vomited water and mud, crawling to the bank while McCracken was dragged away, his face still murderous.

Then Long Bob Handy and his men arrived.

Through a red haze, the only person Lawton saw was Abby Daniels, struggling in Handy's grip.

Moments later, the world tilted violently and he fell off into cold, black space.

CHAPTER 11

OLD GOLD

Lawton felt he had seen all this before.

Once again he was a prisoner of Bob Handy and Abe McCracken. Abby was also a prisoner but kept separate. Wayne was there, tied up, and the way he was being treated did not augur well for his future.

It seemed to Lawton that Handy and McCracken simply didn't know what to do with him, though he would bet they had both thought about how they could use him to persuade Lawton to do what they wanted.

And just what the hell was that?

Simple enough: it was his saddle that had contained the rich gold-nuggets. Therefore either he must know where they came from, or he could lead them to the Indians who gave them to him, and *they* would know.

Trouble was, the Black Hills were crawling with Indians at this time. Custer, back in '74-'75, had violated all treaties by leading in an expedition,

121

searching for and finding the rumoured rich gold deposits that Congress didn't want people to know about – yet.

A railroad to service the Black Hills was planned. There were rumours it had already been started to the north-west, even *before* it had final approval by Congress.

But the tribes had to be relocated first; turning loose gold-hungry adventurers *before* the tribes were resettled would be leaving the Hills wide open for bloody massacre. And that could do the incumbent political party no good at all.

Hopefully, by then the Army would have enough men in the Territory to nip in the bud any attempt at war by the duped and indignant tribes, even if they joined forces. The railroad would ensure that reinforcements could arrive quickly if needed.

Captain Brodie Hall and his unofficial army patrol would know this, be up to date about happenings planned or already occurring in the Black Hills. McCracken was supposedly working for the cap'n, but was more likely to be working for himself, to make sure he got a big, if not *the* biggest, share of the gold. His loyalty to the cap'n only went so far.

But he had Handy for a pardner, whether he wanted him or not. And, more than likely, only for as long as it suited the outlaw leader.

But Lawton was the dog in the manger: he could lead the others to the Indians who, in turn, could lead them to the gold. Whether they *would* was another matter, but that could be handled if and when the situation arose.

Abby and Wayne Daniels were caught in this web and, despite himself, Lawton felt responsible for their welfare.

'You look like a man who has one of them things called a *conscience*, Lawton,' Handy said abruptly, startling the mustanger, seeing as his own thoughts were edging that way. 'Like you'd feel kinda bad if anythin' was to happen to that gal, right? Or her brother.'

He waited but Lawton merely stared, face blank.

Handy shot a stream of spittle within inches of Lawton's head. 'Hell, off my aim. Need some practice. But later. Right now, I reckon it's time to get somethin' straight between us.'

'That'll be the day,' Lawton said sceptically.

'Mmmm – never know.' Handy squatted before him where he sat propped up against a rock. 'I'll just whisper some sweet nothin's in your ear – kind of a . . . preview of what I'll do or have my men do to the gal. Interested?'

Lawton's eyes were deadly. 'I hope you choke on your words.'

Handy laughed, looked up at McCracken. 'Hear that? He's a damn hard nut to crack.'

'I'll crack him!' gritted Abe McCracken and lifted a boot, ready to slam it into Lawton's side. But Handy stood and pushed him away.

'Leave it!' he said irritably. 'I got it all worked out! I wanna see how he feels about co-operatin' *after* we have a little fun with Miss Uppitty.'

'The only fun you'll have is waiting for the devil to stoke up a fire hot enough to throw you in to,' said

123

Lawton, afraid to look in the girl's direction now. He knew he was powerless to stop Handy.

Judging by the look on Abby's face, she knew, too.

'I can lead you to a mine where they got Indians working for them,' Wayne said, desperation plain in his voice.

'Why the hell would I be interested?'

'They're digging gold out of the mine. There're a lot of Indians, so they should be bringing out a lot.'

Handy frowned. 'Nuggets?'

'I . . . I'm not sure,' Wayne stammered and could have bitten his tongue for not lying outright. It was too late now.

'Hell, we ain't interested in stuff wrapped in ore that has to be separated,' McCracken said, annoyed. 'We want *nuggets*, pure and bright yellow, like Lawton had stuffed his saddle with.'

That drew attention to Chance Lawton again. He remained silent.

'You know this mine he's talkin' about?' Handy asked, indicating Wayne.

'I've heard of it.' He tried to sound reluctant, as if he didn't want to talk about it, because it *might* be the one producing the nuggets. Handy might fall for it. . . .

But Handy looked dubious and McCracken sneered. 'Start on the gal, Bob. He'll tell us what we want to know then, instead of all this pussyfootin'.'

Handy sighed. 'Reckon you're right. You'll have a good view, Lawton. Laredo, bring her over here. You fellers wanna draw straws to see who gets to rip her clothes off, go right ahead; we can wait just a little longer.'

Wayne started cursing but Lawton remained silent, his face murderous. Abby struggled but was too weak to break the grip of the two men holding her. The rest were hurriedly picking stalks of grass to use in the draw: *winner take all.*

Abby's eyes locked on to Lawton's face but while he met her stare briefly, he looked away. *Helpless!*

There was a yell and a wild whoop and the man called Red jumped into the air, kicking his heels together, holding the short straw.

'Yoweeee! I git to undress her! Here I come, darlin'. . . .'

Abby recoiled as the rough, dirty outlaw took off his hat and went through the motions of smoothing down his tangled red hair. The others cheered him on.

He rushed across and Abby's face contorted as she fought futilely. Red paused, licked his lips and ran his palms down his trousers. Then, wiggling his fingers, face congesting, he reached out and grabbed a handful of the blouse material.

'Aw, hell, Red!' Laredo called. 'You cain't climb a ladder from the top! Start at the bottom!'

The others roared, urging Red on. He grinned and dropped to one knee, reaching for the girl's waistband. She managed to kick him in the chest but he was a big man and while he winced, it didn't slow him down. He shook a thick finger in her white face. 'Naughty, naught-teee!'

As he lifted her skirt and reached under, Lawton

125

said loudly,

'Leave her be. I'll take you to the man who gave me the nuggets!'

He watched the fear in her eyes quickly replaced by gratitude, but he didn't feel as if he had done any kind of a good deed. Only postponed what Red had in mind.

Redfoot was a friend of his, and a man didn't knowingly dump trouble in a friend's lap.

Unless he had no choice. Like now.

Redfoot was not a particularly tall warrior but he was muscular and his shoulders were wide and square for a man his age. He wore a simple red headband over raven hair, with only a few strands of silver hanging to his shoulders. He wore a buckskin shirt whose beaded designs and painted symbols commemorated his past brave deeds.

He watched McCracken and Handy lead in the band of riders, who showed their hostile intentions by carrying their rifles openly, butts resting against their thighs.

Other warriors stood outside their lodges close to the lance racks and shields, awaiting instructions from their chief. More than a few had repeating rifles.

Then Redfoot straightened as the men parted and Chance Lawton rode forward, his wrists bound in front of him with a rawhide thong. The old Indian's face remained impassive but there was a query and wariness in his old eyes.

He also saw the girl and the young white man

beside her: their hands were bound, too. He shifted his gaze to Lawton, who stopped his horse a few feet from him.

'Welcome, Owned-By-No-Man,' the Sioux said, lifting his right hand in greeting as he spoke the translation of Lawton's Indian name. 'Do I also welcome your companions?'

Lawton shook his head, dismounted awkwardly and Handy stiffened, knuckles whitening on the hand that gripped his rifle. McCracken shook his head briefly.

'They have their damn rituals,' he muttered sourly. 'Nothin' goes right unless they go through 'em.'

Handy grunted, clearly ill at ease with so many Indians staring stolidly – all within reach of some weapon.

Redfoot changed to the Sioux language as he asked Lawton about the bonds and the clearly unfriendly group.

'Speak American, damn it!' Handy snapped but Chance replied in the Indian tongue and Redfoot, face impassive, drew a knife from a fringed belt-sheath and with one sweep cut the rawhide, freeing Chance's hands.

Handy's rifle came to his shoulder and Lawton stepped in front of Redfoot.

'Hold it, Bob! You can't talk with a Sioux chief with your hands bound. He'll want to smoke a little, too, pass around the *tizwin*—'

'He can pass wind for all I care! You just find out where them nuggets come from – and fast! We got lots of matches and these here bucks couldn't get us all

127

before the whole camp was ablaze. You tell him that. Give him some hurry-up!'

He glanced significantly towards the pale-faced girl.

Lawton explained and Redfoot's expression didn't change. He merely held back the flap of his lodge and motioned Chance inside.

'No you don't!' Handy swung the rifle down but paused as Redfoot spoke to him in Lakota. 'The hell did he say to me?'

'He says you're invited. You too, McCracken.'

McCracken curled a lip. 'I don't go in no Injun's house unless I'm gonna burn it down!'

'You damn fool. He savvies American.'

'Good.' McCracken's eyes blazed at the old chief who motioned Lawton and Handy in, then entered himself. 'Hey! We ain't gonna wait while you enjoy yourself! Get the talk done, Lawton, or you'll smell burnin' in ten minutes! That's your deadline!'

'You damn fool,' Lawton muttered, stepping inside.

It seemed a long ten minutes and McCracken was restless in the saddle, looking around all the time, his men doing the same; no one felt at ease here with the stony-faced warriors watching, standing like statues.

Then Handy came bursting out, followed by Lawton, who seemed amused as he looked up at McCracken.

'You want to tell him, Bob, or will I?'

Handy's rifle lifted and poked Lawton hard in the side. 'You – do – it!'

McCracken and the others were all tensed, sensing the news was not going to be good. Lawton looked at

128

them with a sweeping glance, was hard put to keep from smiling.

'Boys, you're out of luck – by about twenty years.'

'The hell's that mean!' demanded McCracken.

Handy started to speak but Chance Lawton didn't want to miss bringing this news and spoke over him.

'The nuggets didn't come from around here. They were left by an old prospector who'd been tore up by a bear. Redfoot and his tribe nursed him back to health. But he knew he was finished prospecting and fur-hunting, and would have to go live in a town close to medical help from then on. He'd hit a bonanza, and he left half of it with the tribe by way of gratitude.'

'Could've happened, I guess,' admitted McCracken. 'But don't tell me these Injuns don't remember where the old sourdough got the nuggets!'

'Oh, they remember. You see, twenty years ago they lived in a different area, far to the west and north of here. Which was where the old prospector found 'em. Like a lot of other tribes they followed the migration of the buffalo herds, and ended up here in the Black Hills.'

Silence, except for a quiet creaking of saddle leather as men moved restlessly, trying to absorb what Lawton was telling them.

'It's old gold, McCracken, literally – but not from around here. No one knows for sure where it came from.'

'You can't tell me the Injuns just kept it all that time!'

'They did. They don't have much use for gold.

129

Make a few necklets maybe, for their women, a button for a belt. No, it just rested there among Redfoot's things. The tribe kind of adopted me and after I managed to save that buck from the buffalo stampedes they decided I could make some use of the gold. I had in mind to buy myself a horse ranch, some time. So they gave it to me.'

It was a hard thing to swallow but McCracken had to hold himself in, the same as did Handy when he'd first been told in Redfoot's lodge. There were too many warriors, too ready to meet any trouble the white men might start.

'We don't have to believe the old bastard,' said Red.

'Indians don't lie as easily as white men,' Lawton told the outlaw curtly. 'Redfoot's telling the truth.'

McCracken glanced at Handy who, tight-lipped, nodded slowly. 'Yeah. I think it was gospel. Don't want to believe it, but. . . .'

'Mebbe we can search?' Laredo suggested, but he cringed at the look McCracken threw him.

'You think they'd let us?' He gestured to the vigilant warriors. McCracken glared, then said coldly, 'I guess we don't have no more use for you, Lawton. Or the Daniels!'

'Makes us lucky.'

'I wouldn't say that! You'll find out when we clear this stink-hole.'

Chance smiled. 'Reckon not. You're in my bailiwick now, McCracken. You didn't think about that when you had me bring you here, did you? Just the gold. You go. We'll stay.'

Handy and McCracken stiffened. There were murmurings from the other outlaws, Red and Laredo edging their horses closer to the Daniels' mounts.

'Like hell!' growled Handy. 'You're comin' with us – and now!'

He lifted his Winchester – or started to. Suddenly he jumped back as there was a dull *clang* and a stone struck the rifle barrel, jarring it out of his hands. A young Indian, barely blooded enough to be called a warrior, stood there with a sling in his hands, his pouch already reloaded.

Long Bob Handy rubbed his tingling hands and raked his now worried gaze around the Indian camp, before turning to McCracken. 'What now?'

McCracken was seething, his hands white, showing all the straining tendons and bones as he gripped his rifle. His eyes burned into Lawton.

'We've still got the gal and her brother!'

'No. Only looks that way.'

'We've got 'em!'

'Dunno why, McCracken, but I'm saving your life by not flicking my little finger. That's all I have to do and Redfoot'll give the signal and you'll find out one way or t'other if there really are any Happy Hunting Grounds.' He let McCracken digest this for a moment, then added, 'By the way, you recall Ishna-Kobay? 'Mo' or 'Treacle' I think you called him. . . .'

Redfoot's face showed brief animation as he flicked his iron gaze from Chance to the lieutenant, now looking worried as he sat stiffly in his saddle.

He didn't speak and Lawton told him softly, 'He was

Redfoot's brother.'

The chief said something succinct in Lakota and Lawton nodded gently.

'What's he sayin'?' McCracken demanded, having to clear his throat even as he spoke.

'He asks if you're the one who killed Mo.'

'Christ! What'd you tell him?'

Lawton nodded at Redfoot. 'Look at him. What d'you think I told him?'

'God, man! What – what're you doin' to me?'

'Nothing you wouldn't do to me. But I was there when you shot Mo. That makes it my responsibility to bring you to heel.'

McCracken was mighty wary now, kept moving his gaze around, wondering when the Indians were going to grab him. But he felt a tiny surge of hope at Lawton's words.

'Are you sayin' . . . you and me go at it, head to head?'

Lawton smiled, shaking his head. 'It's not that easy. But you get a fighting chance. Pardon me if I say that'll be me!'

'Spell it out, damn you?'

Chance had a short discussion with Refoot in Lakota, the old chief making staccato interjections, curt hand gestures. He didn't seem all that pleased, but eventually nodded.

'Yeah, he agrees. You can make a run for it, and I'll be the one to come after you. Only one of us'll come back. How's that suit you?'

CHAPTER 12

NO ESCAPE

It was stifling in among the tall trees.

Sweat had already soaked Lawton's shirt. His hair was wet, so was the buckskin band tied around it, painted with Sioux symbols. He wore half-leg moccasins, for regular cowboy riding-boots would be next to useless in this terrain. He wore no gunbelt, only a stag-handled knife in a sheath pushed round towards the middle of his back.

McCracken was similarly armed.

This was a vengeance hunt and had to be settled man on man, hand to hand, no guns; no bringing down the quarry at 200 yards or more with a flatnosed .44/40 bullet. Not even six-guns, even though such a square-off might be considered acceptable. It would be to white men, of course, but this was red man's rules.

Cold steel, or throttling hands, even a skull-crushing rock – all were allowable. The killer would either die at the hands of the avenger, or kill his opponent and make his escape.

A second avenger would be waiting, though. Should the quarry kill *him*, a third man would take his place. . . .

The murderer would know by then there was no esacpe. He would be run down and killed: the longer it took, the more horrible his own death.

There was the red man's version of honour here.

Lieutenant McCracken had looked grey when this was explained to him at Redfoot's camp.

'Christ! Why don't they just kill me now and be done with it!'

'Too easy,' Chance Lawton told him, honing his knife. He held it up and sun flashed from the slightly curving blade. 'This belonged to Ishna-Kobay. It's what'll kill you, McCracken.'

'Not with you usin' it!' But it was bravado and everyone within hearing knew it.

Abby Daniels looked tense and worried as Lawton, apparently casually, made preparations. 'It's – barbaric, Chance,' she told him but without real reproach.

'So's shooting a man in the back in cold blood.'

There was no answer to that and Wayne said, 'Is there a notebook or something handy?' At his sister's cold look, he added, 'Sis, this will make one helluva article for *On Watch*.'

Tight-lipped, she jerked her head in a nod. 'I have a tally book in my saddle-bag, if you want to get it.'

He grinned, moving quickly towards her tethered horse. 'Thanks, Sis.'

Minutes later, McCracken was gone.

Two hard-eyed braves led his horse downslope, away from the camp, past all the staring whites, and disappeared into the trees and boulders.

It was forty minutes before they came back, leading McCracken's riderless horse. Redfoot touched Lawton on the shoulder and he sprinted out of the camp, Indians yelling encouragement, waving lances and guns and tomahawks. It unsettled Handy and his men, who only wanted to get out of here alive. And that was by no means certain.

Wayne wrote furiously in the tally book and Abby found she was holding her breath.

Lawton knew where McCracken had been left by the warriors and his starting out on foot was designed to give the quarry a chance to make his preparations, either for an ambush or total escape. The latter, of course, was not possible but it would be only human nature to attempt it.

Lawton knew the country, took short cuts that he was able to, being on foot, which a man on horseback would have to pass up.

That was why Abe McCracken had such a shock when, panting from climbing a large egg-shaped boulder so he could get a better view, he saw movement down by a creek that he had crossed not twenty minutes earlier.

It was Lawton, running well, in that deceptively

135

easy, distance-eating stride of the Indian warrior who could keep up such a pace all day – and well into the night.

'Goddamn! If I only had a gun!' McCracken gritted.

But he could make preparations, anyway. He cast about him and found a heavy dead branch like a bent arm, the wood almost petrified. There were rocks of handy size nearby, too. . . .

He grinned tightly. 'Come on, Lawton! I'm waitin'.'

He was still waiting twenty minutes later, his guts tied in a knot, head spinning, eyes burning from straining to see.

Where the hell had he gone!

By now Chance ought to have been in the area below the huge rock, but there had been no sign of him since that brief sighting down by the creek.

He *had* to come this way if he wanted to get over the ridge. It would take him an hour or more to skirt it, unless – unless he knew some other way not obvious to McCracken!

His mouth was dry as dust as he edged forward, clutching his club, making sure a pile of fist-sized rocks were close to hand. Carefully, he inched up to the edge of the boulder and looked over, very, very nervously.

Hell, he had been fighting goddam Injuns for twelve years. He had once started taking scalps but everyone complained about the stink and he lost count just trying to remember those he'd killed. They had come in their dozens. He had *enjoyed* the battle, looked forward to it.

Then why the hell was he so churned up over this – just one man, and not even a fullblood!

The answer was simple: he had his guns then, was backed by his well-armed troop. Here he was alone and had to make do with primitive weapons that he had to improvise.

There was a light thud behind him and McCracken spun on to his back, feeling his breath stop. *Judas priest!* His heart almost stopped, too!

Lawton was a few feet away, just straightening from his leap down on to the top of the boulder. He didn't even have his knife drawn. His face was red and running with sweat from his exertions and he was breathing heavily but steadily.

McCracken scrabbled to grab a rock and hurled it wildly. Chance dodged easily and the killer launched himself headlong, swiping at Lawton's legs with the club. If the blow had landed it would have broken the leg, but Chance leapt over the weapon and landed closer to the now sprawling killer.

He swung his right foot, grunting with effort, his toes hurting as the moccasin drove brutally into McCracken's ribs. The army man groaned aloud and spun away towards the edge.

Chance strode after him and caught him another blow in the armpit. McCracken's legs went over the edge and he twisted, fingers trying to dig into the rough rock for a hold. Chance stomped on the hand and McCracken yelled as he fell a dozen feet, twisting in mid-air. He hit the sloping ground just clear of the boulder's base and slid down through the dirt, raising

137

a cloud of dust and dead leaves.

Lawton crouched on the rock's edge, waiting for the other to come to a standstill. McCracken rammed his boots against a tree and spun around, lying there, gasping, spitting grit.

Until Chance started bombarding him with the rocks he had left piled up on top of the boulder.

Then he hurled himself behind the tree, stayed there a few moments, then started running, still managing to hold his crooked club.

Chance Lawton clambered down, sliding and staggering on the slope, running involuntarily, slapping at tree trunks not only to slow his progress to give him more control, but so that he angled off to his right.

There was no sign of McCracken but, stopping to lean against a tree, swallowing, trying to ease his panting, Lawton strained to hear. Yeah! Below, about halfway between the ridge and creek where the trees and brush were thickest, he heard McCracken crashing his way north, which was the only way he could go to take him away from Redfoot's camp.

He rested to let his heart and breathing get in order, then picked his way down to the flat, heading towards the bend of the creek. McCracken had stopped to drink: the grass at the edge and some of the soil was wet where he had gulped and splashed water. Chance knelt and sucked up a mouthful, swirling it around his mouth before swallowing.

It would see him through for now; no sense in trying to run with a gallon of water sloshing around in your belly.

McCracken was learning, or remembering his army training. He deliberately broke twigs on bushes, making it look as though he had gone in that direction, while he had really gone the opposite way. Those army boot-tracks were hard to hide and Chance had little trouble picking up the man's real trail.

But he was fit, that murderous lieutenant, and the chase went on well into the afternoon, surprising Lawton. He wanted to be out of these trees before sundown, while McCracken would likely prefer to stay in their midst and set his ambushes in the dark.

The army man was staying away from the ground where dead leaves and twigs would give away his position. It was a sign that he was planning an ambush, which meant he had to lure Lawton to the place.

So when Chance heard a scraping sound like a man staggering or stumbling over an area of dead twigs, he froze. McCracken had deliberately made that sound, maybe dragging a dead branch at the end of a vine while he crouched hidden amongst the trees. He would expect Lawton to come to investigate.

So that was what Chance did, or made enough noise to suggest he was hurrying towards the sound. He threw some dead branches into the brush so as to make a noise that might indicate a man thrusting his way through, in a hurry to catch his prey before dark.

In his moccasins, noiseless the way he placed his feet, he angled in towards the position he figured McCracken would be. The shadows were deepening in here now, and he had to rely on his hearing just as much as his vision. Dropping to one knee, with the sunlit edge of the trees ahead, he bent way down, looked across the forest floor. He was lucky enough to find where the leaves and twigs had been pushed up in little waves, from McCracken's branch tied to a vine to make the sound that was intended to confuse his pursuer.

He started to straighten, working out which side of the trees he would approach from, when there was a tremendous crash beside his head and he staggered as splinters tore at the right side of his face and ear. It was McCracken's bent club. The man had thrown it at him and almost succeeded in braining him, but it had shattered against a tree trunk.

It must have come from behind and slightly above.

McCracken had outwitted him, waited higher upslope than Chance had allowed for.

He just had time to have these thoughts when there was a crashing like a mustang bursting through the brush and he spun, awkwardly in his half-crouch. McCracken's arms wrapped around him and the man's head drove into his midriff.

It was like being hit by a runaway train.

Breath exploded out of him and his legs folded as McCracken's sheer weight and impact drove him over backwards. He went down – and clawed his fingers into McCracken's broad shoulders, dragging the man with him.

The lieutenant hadn't expected that and he spilled to one side. His head struck the ground and stars burst behind his eyes. He grunted and his right arm arced across and down. Light winked off naked steel and Chance heaved and spun under the other's weight. The blade drove into the ground, stone tinkling against the metal. Upper body twisted, Chance was in the right position to use his elbow.

He brought his left arm back hard, felt the jar as the elbow thudded against his opponent's temple or jaw. McCracken sagged and Lawton kicked free, drove both moccasins into the snarling face. Abe's head snapped back and blood spurted as his lips crushed against his teeth. He rolled, looping one arm about Lawton's still extended legs. He hung on, tucking them into his armpit as he roared to his feet with a mighty effort, bringing most of Chance's body with him. But the mustanger was upside down, his head still on the ground. McCracken spun, trying to break his neck.

Gravel tore at Chance's face and one ear and he felt warm blood flowing. But he managed to get enough slack in his legs to snap them straight, catching the other man unawares. McCracken tried to keep his footing but his leather boots slipped in the loose gravel and on the dead and half-green twigs under the soles. He flailed, releasing the legs and stumbled like a two-jug drunk, desperately trying to stay on his feet.

Chance was dazed and blood masked his face. Irritably, he wiped it out of his eyes, saw the killer within reach and lashed out, right and left, knuckles crunching and splitting flesh as McCracken's head snapped back as if it would fly off his shoulders. Chance crowded him across the slope relentlessly, bulling forward, taking several hard blows in retalia-

141

tion now but ignoring them.

The army man knew he was hurting the mustanger and with renewed vigour set his boots in the ground and braced his shoulders, arms ready to piston in on Lawton's midriff. Chance danced back, slipped and put down an arm to keep from falling completely. A boot took him in the left shoulder, right beside his jaw, twisted him and sent him flailing back, arms flying out for balance. He went down most of the way, then McCracken was on him, boots slamming, towering over the doubled-up Lawton, hammering blows to his spine and kidneys. Chance went down to one knee, gasping, head hanging, a string of blood dribbling from his mouth and hanging six inches below his jawline. His head was roaring and the darkening woods seemed to be rippling and moving, like shadowy warriors on a night raid.

The knife was out again.

He realized this only when the blade sliced through loose folds of his shirt and he felt a searing pain across his ribs as the honed edge cut him.

He wasn't quite sure what he did, but somehow he spun and hooked a heel into one of McCracken's kneecaps. The leg gave way and the lieutenant went down on one knee. But he slashed wildly back-handed as Chance slowed and the mustanger leapt back just in time.

Then his own knife was in his hand, the rough, shaped stag handle gripped firmly even though his hand was slippery with sweat. McCracken's teeth were bared as he lunged up from his knees, favouring the leg with the throbbing kneecap, and he threw himself forward, knife blade held out in front of him.

Chance twisted quickly to one side, brought his knife hand around in a wide, looping arc that stopped abruptly. And suddenly his hand was wet with something warm and sticky. He couldn't free the blade, so he twisted violently and jumped back as McCracken screamed.

The army man swayed on his knees, his knife lying on the ground, his eyes wide and staring, both hands pressed into his chest as he tried to dislodge Chance's blade, which jammed in the cartilage of his sternum, penetrating his heart. With a massive dying effort he freed the blade and air blasted through the wound with a high-pitched screeching, whistling sound. Dark arterial blood spurted.

His body fell forward, his boots drumming briefly.

By then, Chance Lawton was sitting down, knees drawn up, head resting against his forearms.

'Rest easy now, Mo. Rest easy, old friend.'

It was dark and still there was no sign of Chance Lawton returning to the camp.

The Indians had cooking-fires burning, and a larger one on a rise, a kind of beacon.

Redfoot and some of his council sat around their own fire, the *shaman* chanting quietly, occasionally sprinkling some noxious-smelling powder over the coals.

Long Bob Handy and the other outlaws were off to one side, crowded together; three warriors were on watch. They were given food but most spat it out.

'Goddamn Injun grub! It'd make a billy-goat puke!' was the general opinion.

Abby and Wayne nibbled but were unable to eat the half-cooked meat, whatever it was.

'It doesn't look good, does it,' she said quietly, and Wayne knew she was not referring to the meal.

He glanced up, forced a smile. 'He's a mighty tough man, Sis.'

'But McCracken is a cold-blooded murderer!'

Wayne just stopped himself from saying that Lawton wasn't much better: whites might have partly raised him, but it seemed to Wayne that Lawton's Indian upbringing had the most influence.

Then there was a rising series of cries and she saw the Indians standing up one by one down at their big fire.

'Someone's coming!' Abby said tautly, and jumped to her feet.

Wayne stood quickly. Handy and his men were watching closely, too.

A lone, bloody, ragged figure staggered into the Indian camp.

'Oh! It's Chance!' Abby breathed in immense relief. 'Look at the welcome they're giving him!'

The Indians were crowding around Lawton, lit by the flames of the beacon fire. Bob Handy nodded in a prearranged signal. His men converged on the warrior guards who were watching Lawton's return. In seconds the Indians were stretched out unconscious and the outlaws started to move away towards the picket line of horses, in a hollow down the other slope.

Handy hesitated, glancing at the Daniels, but they had moved closer to the Indian camp and he decided to hell with them: they were of little use to him now.

While they quietly got their mounts, Abby and Wayne stopped at the edge of the camp and saw Lawton clearly.

He was obviously hurt, judging by the amount of blood on him, but he was on his feet and talking animatedly to the querying braves.

'What's that he's holding?' Abby asked and Wayne squinted.

'Looks like a cap of some kind. Maybe a furry animal, I don't know. But I want to talk with him, Sis, get his story.'

He started forward, stopped when her hand closed tightly on his arm.

When she spoke there was a touch of horror in her voice.

'Dear God! It's a scalp!'

CHAPTER 13

LAST PATROL

Long Bob Handy slowed down once they reached the foot of the mountain. His men hauled rein around him, most looking quizzical.

Bob hipped in the saddle, scanning the dark figures of his riders. 'I sure as hell don't take kindly to bein' treated this way by a bunch of Injuns.'

'Well, hell, none of us do, Bob,' said Laredo.

'OK, we're still alive and even got our own mounts and most of our guns.' He tapped his forehead. 'But it's still up here! We was treated like trash – *by goddamn Injuns*!'

Red moved uncomfortably in his saddle. 'Well, I reckon we was lucky to get out alive, Bob. If it hadn't been for Lawton, our scalps'd be hangin' in Redfoot's lodge now.'

Handy reared in his stirrups, glaring at the man. 'And that's the other thing! I can't abide bein' beholden to Chance Lawton!'

'Hell, it ain't anythin' to feel beholden about, Bob. Lawton just didn't want that gal to get hurt, is all. It'd suit us all better if we'd been able to nail him, take the woman and burn the damn camp, but we ain't got enough men.'

The outlaws were quick to agree. It didn't make Handy any happier. 'You wanna run off with your tails between your legs, go back to hittin' stages or trains?'

'We ain't done too bad so far.'

Handy snorted. 'Ain't done all that good neither. The gal's kid brother reckons he can find that other mine, the one with the slavers makin' the Injuns dig for gold. He's still in Redfoot's camp but Jude ought to be on his way back now with the cap'n and his men. Laredo, you and Fuzzy stay and keep an eye on Lawton and the Injuns. Rest of us'll go meet Cap'n Brodie. If we don't find him, we'll have to think of something else.'

'Wish you'd think of somethin' else now,' Laredo moaned unhappily, as the others prepared to ride off.

Chance Lawton looked a lot worse than he was. He had numerous cuts and grazes but only two knife slashes, one in his upper arm, the other across his lower ribs, which Abby said should be stitched. But he was content to allow the medicine man to pin the skin across with thorns.

'That must hurt!' she gasped, as he writhed.

Sweat was beading his brow, which was cut and grazed, too. 'Can't feel a thing!' he gritted with mock bravery.

147

She watched as the old medicine man moved about Lawton's battered body, humming and chanting as he passed his wrinkled hands and eagle feathers over each wound.

'You are mostly Indian, I think, enduring this.'

'Doesn't do any harm, even if not a lot of good.'

Wayne sat in the background, writing furiously in Abby's tally book. Several times he asked Lawton questions about the manhunt and the fight to the death.

'I still think I could find my way back to that slavers' mine,' Wayne said, closing the notebook.

Lawton nodded. 'It's the kind of thing that has to be stopped. Colonel Helm has patrols up this way. If I can get word to him, he'd likely divert one. But it'll be up to the officer in charge whether you're allowed within spitting distance of any raid, Wayne.'

'I'll talk my way in,' Wayne said confidently, winking at Abby. 'I have the gift of the gab, don't I, Sis?'

'You have . . . persistence, Wayne. I'm not sure I like it.'

'Well, Sis, you don't really have to. Do you?'

She felt hurt at his tone, but as he stood and stretched, she realized her 'little' brother had grown into a man: his own man.

And she felt a certain sadness at the knowledge.

Chance Lawton was glad to spend a couple of days in the Indian camp recovering from his wounds and general aches and pains.

It surprised him that he was slower to recover than he had expected, but he realized that now he was in his mid-thirties, as far as anyone could tell, and he'd lived a mighty hard life. Hunting mustangs and breaking them in was not an easy chore and he had been doing it for years now. He had suffered many broken bones and more than once had been stranded with injuries in all kinds of weather.

So he was glad of the excuse to recuperate, and glad of Abby Daniels' company. He had written out a long explanatory message for Colonel Helm down in Fort Savage and Redfoot had had one of his younger sons carry it to the nearest telegraph station at Roughcut, a timber and logging town over the mountain from where the camp was.

Hopefully, if Helm had a patrol handy, he would divert it to Redfoot's camp where Lawton and Wayne could join them on the search for the mine run by slave labour. Wayne busied himself drawing maps of the country as he recalled it and had sent an article by telegraph on the Indian justice dished out to Abe McCracken, murderer of Ishna-Kobay.

Abby found herself fascinated by the Indians; the women had been friendly enough when she asked to watch them go about their chores, but she could see they were not at ease with a white woman.

'When d'you expect to know what Helm's going to do?' Wayne asked Lawton, growing impatient.

'Who knows? If an army patrol comes here we'll know. If it doesn't, we'll have to send someone down to Roughcut and see if there's any reply to the telegraph.'

Wayne smiled thinly. 'I – er – slipped a couple of

dollars into an envelope for the telegrapher. He'll send a man here as soon as there's anything from Helm.'

'Can't wait, can you?'

'It's my big chance – Chance. That name of yours can be awkward at times! I feel if I can pull this off. . . .'

Lawton held up a hand as a young Indian lad he knew as 'Little Frog' came and stood to one side.

Lawton spoke in Lakota, asked him what he wanted and the boy answered rapidly and excitedly, pointing to the low ridge.

'What is it?' Wayne asked.

'One of their scouts has seen an army patrol heading this way. So it looks like we were lucky and Helm had some men close by.'

Wayne's eyes lit up. 'Then we'll be going to the other mine! That's very good news, Chance! I'll get my first-hand, on-the-spot story of a military operation in the Black Hills! It'll be a first and *On Watch* will not only pay big, but offer me a job there!'

'Calm down, man! It's all up to the army officer now. Wait till they get here before you start counting your chickens.'

But Wayne couldn't contain himself. He went in search of his sister, who was off with the women, dyeing their yarn to be woven into colourful blankets.

Lawton stood and stretched, ground out his cigarette under foot and picked up the Winchester rifle he had been cleaning and oiling.

Someone called and he looked up to where Little Frog was standing on top of a high boulder on the ridge with two other youths in breechclouts, holding bows and arrows.

'They come!' the boy called in his piping voice. Lawton hurried across and rested the rifle against the base of the rock, found foot- and toe-holds and climbed up laboriously.

Panting harder than he expected, Chance Lawton straightened a little stiffly and looked disdainfully at one of the boys who offered him a thin helping hand.

He stepped up beside the excited Little Frog. The youth pointed down into the trees where the trail wound back and forth.

Chance shaded his eyes, glimpsing the uniforms, trying to see how many men there were. Then he stiffend.

'Judas Priest! That's not Helm's men! It's Captain Brodie Hall's crew and – Goddammit! There's Bob Handy and his men riding with 'em!'

He almost fell in his hurry to get down. He snatched up the rifle, meaning to fire a couple of shots to warn Redfoot and his men, then realized the gun was still unloaded.

Swearing, all stiffness and aches forgotten, he sprinted towards the main section of the camp, yelling:

'We're under attack! We're. . . .'

The words choked back in his throat as he saw a second column making its way down from the high ridge, spreading out on the almost treeless slopes. Jude Hall was leading, throwing a rifle to his shoulder even as Lawton watched. They were coming in from both sides, covering the two exit trails.

Then the first shots and screams tore through the early afternoon, as a hail of bullets cut down women and children gathered around a hide-stretching frame, where there was a demonstration of removing the last fat-globules.

Warriors were running everywhere now, back and forth, criss-crossing the camp ground. Two tumbled and fell rolling, lying still when they came to a halt. Another reeled, staggered, but managed to keep his balance and dive through the opening of a tepee. A young woman, hugging a papoose tightly to her breast ran for the scrub. A rider broke away from the main line of attackers, put his mount after her, rode her into the ground. Then he spun the wild-eyed mount about and drew his pistol, shooting coldly.

Lawton skidded under the skirt of the tepee that had been allocated to him, snatched at his six-gun rig and knelt while he buckled it about his waist. He picked up a handful of rifle cartridges and began pushing them through the loading gate. He fumbled three times, then made himself calm down.

Several bullets tore through the hide of the tent and he ducked involuntarily just as a bearded white man tore the entrance wide open and lurched in, smoking six-gun in hand. He swung the weapon towards Lawton who rolled on to his side and triggered the rifle twice. The lead drove the bearded man back and down.

Chance was up and leaping over the quivering body, into the open. It was a butcher's shop: riders yelling and shouting, shooting indiscriminately. He saw an old woman's thin leg smashed out from under her by a bullet. He twisted to find the shooter, but a raider came out of nowhere and tried to ride him under.

Chance shoulder-rolled, thrust the rifle up and felt the muzzle jab under the man's ribs as he leaned from the saddle. The sound of the shot was muffled and the man's body lifted six inches off his horse before tumbling. Lawton grabbed the flying reins, threw his weight back to slow the snorting black, then leapt into the saddle.

He couldn't see Abby or even Wayne. A shadow fell across him and he wrenched his body around as one of Captain Brodie Hall's 'soldiers' slashed at him with a sabre. Chance parried the blow with the barrel of the Winchester, gripped the horse tightly with his knees, and drew his six-gun, shooting into the man's contorted face.

The black was wild and excited under him and he fought it with reins and knees and even shouted words. Dust and gunsmoke were thick, blinding clouds were swirling through the camp. Flames appeared blurred through the fog. The screams of women and children, and some of mortally wounded men, mingled with the crash of gunfire, the thudding hoofs and the cursing of the raiders.

He saw Redfoot, standing outside his lodge, raising an old shotgun some Scotsman had given him in exchange for a decorated buckskin shirt. A man in one of Brodie Hall's ragged uniforms tried desperately to wheel aside, but the charge of buckshot caught him above the hip and blew him completely out of the saddle.

As Redfoot broke open the breech to reload he suddenly staggered, cannoned into one of the sapling uprights of the lodge and fell back to sit down hard. There was blood on his rugged face and his mouth hung slackly.

Lawton took this in in seconds. He whirled in the saddle, holding the rifle in one hand. He saw the man who had shot Redfoot closing in to finish off the old chief. Triggering the rifle one-handed made the barrel jump and the bullet meant for the man's torso took him in the head.

The Winchester was empty now. As he crashed his black into another horse, Chance lost the rifle in the ensuing tangle. He tried to reach down for it but missed, then the black staggered as a bullet took it in the body, just above Lawton's leg.

He tumbled out of the saddle, hit the ground hard, breath bursting from him, his sight momentarily distorted. He rolled and skidded half-under the buckskin skirt of a tepee. Continuing to roll, he pushed to his feet and ran to the entrance, saw the rider coming at him full tilt.

It was Jude Hall. The man's face was contorted, his hands were working the lever of a heavy-calibre rifle.

He rode straight into the tepee lodge, sending Chance staggering and tumbling into a corner. There was a squaw huddling there with two little girls. She was screaming along with the children.

Lawton hurled himself at the wall, ripping a way out through bullet holes with the foresight of the Colt, tangling in the rent hide, falling over part of the sapling frame.

Jude came surging after him, shooting. The big gun – a trapdoor Springfield – thundered and the bullet shattered the hand-thick sapling like matchwood. But it was only a single shot and Jude fumbled the reload trying to push it into the trapdoor breech.

Lawton jerked to his feet and threw himself at the man bodily. They crashed out of the saddle and rolled outside the half-collapsed tepee. Fists and knees thudded and hammered and Chance kicked Jude away, sending him stumbling. Jude came up with a Remington pistol gripped in both hands. Lawton dived headlong, triggering as he did so. He was lower than Jude and the bullet travelled upward, taking Jude under the jaw.

Panting, half-blinded by dust and stinging gun-smoke, Lawton thumbed shells from his belt loops and pushed them into the hot cylinder of the Colt.

'Now that's what I call real luck! Findin' you!'

Crouching, cylinder only half-loaded, Chance froze at the sound of the voice.

Long Bob Handy stood some three yards away, legs spread, rifle butt braced into his hip, finger on the trigger. His hat was askew and blood trickled down his face. There was more blood on his shirtfront but he was still fighting mad. He spat a stream of spittle that fell just short of Lawton but he pulled back his lips, revealing the large gap in his mouth as he raised the rifle's barrel just a little. His knuckle whitened on the trigger.

Chance's shot went straight through that huge gap in Handy's teeth.

The camp was burning in places and suddenly there were horses and men everywhere, going in the one direction, frantically heading for the trail that led into the hills.

Lawton blinked his stinging eyes as he saw men in almost clean blue uniforms charging after the fleeing raiders, or what was left of them. The hats were standard but had a newish look and he knew that this was the real army patrol: Helm's men, genuine soldiers.

As he watched, standing there with the smoking Colt down at his side, an officer rode up, his face greasy with smoke and grit. He nodded, eyes showing white against the grime.

'Still getting yourself into more trouble than you can handle, Chance?'

Lawton grinned. 'I don't need to worry; you always seem to be close by, Wes.'

Lieutenant Wes Paisley dismounted and grunted a little, rubbing an aching hip as he holstered his pistol and offered his right hand to Lawton. They gripped hands.

'You always did have more than your share of luck, you damn 'breed.' The last was said affectionately, and at Chance's quizzical look, Paisley said, 'The telegraph man was still sending your wire to Colonel Helm when my patrol rode into Roughcut for extra supplies. So we came straight here.'

'Damn glad you did. See the captain?'

'Old Brodie? Oh, yes, grabbed him early on. Too slow these days, but he'll get his chance to rest up. Got him down the hill chained to the wheel of our chuckwagon. Big trial waiting for him and Lacy. They won't see real daylight for about twenty years.' Paisley sobered and looked around him. He raised his voice. 'Doctor! Sawbones! Over here! Some women and kids hurt in this tepee. Sergeant, get your crew dousing that fire. For God's sake, you want the whole blamed mountain to go up in smoke?'

Lawton grinned and clapped Paisley on the back. 'I'll leave you to it.'

'As usual.' Paisley looked beyond Chance's shoulder and smiled wryly. 'Ah. yes. I see you have something more . . . interesting to attend to.'

Lawton turned curiously and found Abby Daniels coming towards him, her clothes filmed with dirt and blood. Other people's, as it turned out; her hair was hanging across her forehead, she pushed it back and gave him a smile.

'I think I shall head back to my ranch. It's much more peaceful there.'

'Are you all right?'

Her smile widened. 'You sound concerned. Yes, thank you, I'm all right. But there's a lot more to be done here before nightfall. I'm looking for something to boil some water in.'

He pointed to an overturned iron pot outside a burning lodge, then started to hurry across the littered ground. 'Talk to you later.'

She frowned, suddenly saw where he was going. Redfoot was propped up against a tree, his face bloody. A *shaman* was making signs and chanting invocations to the Great Spirit, others were bandaging his legs.

'Redfoot. . . ?'

The chief raised his eyes to Lawton. 'I – must wait a while yet – before I meet the Great – Spirit, Owned-By-No-Man.'

'Glad to hear that. Some of your warriors have already gone to the Happy Hunting Grounds.'

'They died bravely.'

It was his way of saying that it was the warrior's way: death held no fear for such men. To die fighting an enemy was what every true warrior wished for.

Later, after supper around a huge campfire with the army cook dishing out barbecued meat of various kinds, Lawton sat on a log beside Abby, chewing on a cutlet. On the other side Wayne was busy writing up his recollections of the battle in the well-used tally-book, scratching and scribbling as he searched for the words and phrases he wanted. He was trying hard to finish his article before he was due to lead Paisley's patrol in the search for the mine run by slave labour; he was looking forward to it: yet another first-hand account under his byline. He would be famous overnight.

Lawton wiped his fingers on some cloth the girl handed him, asked quietly, 'When do you leave for Wyoming?'

'Fairly soon, I think.' She looked at him speculatively. 'I'm planning a trail drive down to Cheyenne, and I'll need about – oh, forty, fifty horses for the remuda. Could you supply them?'

He looked at her soberly, nodded slowly. 'I could. Take quite a while to break in that many, though.'

'Yes, I know,' she said casually, giving him a half-smile. After a pause she said, 'I'll be needing a wrangler for the drive itself, there and back. And I'm planning on expanding so I'll probably have to bring in more stock for the ranch after that. Or, perhaps I could contract you to supply me, long term, with horses as necessary?' Her smile widened, warm and encouraging. 'Would you be interested at all?'